Another Time, Another Place

Ann T. Keene

iUniverse, Inc.
New York Bloomington

Another Time, Another Place

This is a work of fiction. All of the characters, names, incidents, organizations, and dialogue in this novel are either the products of the author's imagination or are used fictitiously.

iUniverse books may be ordered through booksellers or by contacting:

iUniverse
1663 Liberty Drive
Bloomington, IN 47403
www.iuniverse.com
1-800-Authors (1-800-288-4677)

ISBN: 978-1-4502-2357-7 (sc)
ISBN: 978-1-4502-2358-4 (ebk)

Printed in the United States of America

iUniverse rev. date: 5/17/2010

For Juanita Schoff,
with gratitude and love.

If the heart could think, it would stop beating.

Fernando Pessoa, *The Book of Disquiet*

Contents

Chloë, in the Morning of Her Life

Memory begins like this:

"Don't forget her panties."

Da speaking, though Mother, who won't be called anything else, says she must address him as Father.

By the kitchen door, filling his pipe, Da mashes down tobacco with a little silver nail, then pulls a book of matches from his pocket and strikes a light. The matchbook says Simms Electric, which is where Da worked before they moved here. There are lots of these matches in one of the kitchen drawers; Mother uses them to light the oven. At the moment Mother lies mute in the big bedroom down the hall, blackout shades drawn tight.

Chloë closes her own bedroom door and comes into the kitchen. She is wearing underpants, see? she says, holding up her blue pinafore to show Da. She put them on herself, taking them out of the suitcase that holds her underwear in the corner of the small bedroom. Last week Mother sent her out without them, she had no clean ones, saying no one would notice though of course they did.

Out they go onto the landing, and Da stops to fiddle with the pipe that won't stay lit. The Neales' door across the way is closed, against intruders perhaps, or maybe they aren't home now, though Chloë saw them this morning, sitting on her little stool outside and watching through the screen while they ate breakfast and talked. All of them, the big Neales, Mr. and Mrs., and one of the boys, Don. He and his brother, Jerry, are big, too, but still live at home, at least Don does. Jerry is a soldier, a Marine, away at war. All well and good, says Mother. She prefers Don.

Chloë shuffles her feet with impatience. It's hot on the landing, even in seersucker, sandals, and thin panties, and the treat of blowing out each match that Da strikes is wearing thin. They do this every Saturday, walk to the park three streets away, three *squares*, says Da, with swings and a merry-go-round that Da can't push very hard and benches for Da to sit on while Chloë goes down the slide and squirrels that beg for the Black Crows that Da buys for her to eat without Mother's knowledge. They spend a long time at the park, so that Mother can nap before dinner. Mother was sick when it was still cold outside, sick in a way Chloë doesn't understand, though she remembers lots of blood on the kitchen floor one afternoon and Mother slumped in a chair, telling her to get Mrs. Neale. Mother is still not well, says Da. She needs her rest.

Now the pipe flames, and Da puffs a stream of rings. Chloë blows out one last match and walks downstairs taking Da's hand, the left one because the right has a little finger tightly arced into a C, its tight skin an opaque pale yellow, like the bakelite dresser set on Mother's bureau. There is something horrible about the finger, like the witch's hands in *Snow White*, and she doesn't like to touch it. *As a young man*, many years ago it must have been because Da looks like an old one now, with wrinkles and thin grey hair and drooping eyes, *Father broke a piece of fishing line and cut his hand. It got infected because he did not wash it with soap and water, and then it grew into an ugly shape.* Mother has said this many times, often in Da's hearing, though he says nothing. He does not voice objection to her telling, though she is blaming him for an accident not his fault, or so thinks Chloë. That story, like so many of Mother's, is meant to be a lesson.

They pass other closed doors on their way downstairs, behind which live the Morgans and their dog Duke, the Schneiders who speak only German, a family named Click with an invalid daughter, Aunt Lucille who isn't really her aunt. On the first floor are the dry cleaning man and his wife, Italians they call Mr. and Mrs. Gravy, and Mr. O'Connor, an old man who takes care of the building. Chloë knows them all by heart, but she knows the Neales best of all because they live across the hall. She has watched them ever since she and Mother and Da moved here, which is almost as far back as she remembers. It was warm then, too, but not for long, though after the days grew cold Mrs. Neale sometimes left her porch door open. And then it was Christmas, and Mr. and Mrs. gave her candy and showed her their big tree with a blue-robed angel on top, and then Easter, with a special basket, wrapped in purple cellophane, just for her from Mr. Neale, who owns a big drugstore in South Shore that sells chocolate eggs. Mother ate the eggs; chocolate isn't good for children, she said.

And now it is August, almost September, still so very hot, even for Chicago, Mrs. Neale has said more than once to Mother, whom she like everyone else calls Mrs. Mack. Mother did not grow up in Chicago, so Mrs. Neale tells her things about the city she thinks Mother doesn't know. Mack is Da's nickname so Mother gets it, too, though she tells people she's Mrs. Vincent. It is 1944, and Chloë, old as the decade, begins to have memories.

They moved to South Shore, said Mother, because it was a nicer place. Meaning that it was better than the hotel room near the lake where they'd been living since Chloë was born. Furniture came with the new apartment, a table and chairs for the dining room and a bed for Mother and Da and dressers and a stuffed chair and sofa covered with green stripes like an awning. And chipped plates with roses on them and glasses cloudy with age and dented kitchen pots. For decoration two Wallace Nutting tinted photographs, similar views of an apple orchard, framed in gilded bronze. And a desk for Mother, with a bar at one end to put the bottles of sweet wine she drank in the afternoon, for a headache she said. The other end of the desk had a locked drawer, deep enough to hold lots of secrets.

Sometime before they moved, Da bought these things from the people who lived in the apartment then, a man and his wife and their little boy Peter, who had only an angry red blob of scarred tissue for a left ear. Chloë had come along with Mother and Da, there being no place where they could leave her, and Da suggested that they play downstairs in the front courtyard, she and Peter, while the grown-ups had their talk. But she hadn't wanted to go anywhere with Peter, who made strange sounds that only his parents could understand. A birth defect, said Mother later in the taxi, lighting up a Herbert Tareyton. A few days later another taxi took the three of them and their suitcases and Mother's trunk and several cardboard boxes tied with brown string away from the hotel and drove them to the apartment again, this time for good. Da carried her stool, made of wood painted with red and yellow flowers. Da had bought it for Chloë when she had her tonsils out. Chloë sat on a little round foldout seat in the back of the taxi, holding a bear named Ambrose. Mother named the bear, a present from the hotel maid. Mother had names and reasons for everything. Chloë slept on the awning sofa for a few days, and then Da found her a little folding bed on Maxwell Street.

"Mrs. Mack, you simply have no idea . . . ," says Don, sharing another sly outrage with Mother. He tilts his head upward and releases clouds of bluish haze from small pinched nostrils. Don smokes Camels in a filter he says is made of ivory. He's chatting with Mother at the kitchen table, all dressed up, as Mother later reports to Da, in a starched white shirt and navy suit and matching silk bowtie with white polka dots. Across from him sits Mother, an apron hanging loosely over her housedress, pulling strings from green beans and snapping them into a pot. Chloë is on her stool in the corner by the stove, pretending to play with Ambrose. Mother's Herbert Tareyton burns at her elbow on a large crystal ashtray. She pauses to take a puff.

"Donald," she says, blowing smoke toward Chloë. "I think you're making this up," a sly smile and rolled eyes belying disbelief.

Don is often in their kitchen, drinking coffee and gossiping. He goes to the university, only a few miles away, one of the youngest students there. He graduated at seventeen, and now he's working on a master's degree in something to do with politics. He's old enough now to be in the war but has been exempted. *Four-F,* Mother and Da whispered to each other, Da with a knowing look, Mother with what appeared to be sympathy. When the subject came up with Mrs. Neale, normally self-assured and now vulnerable, Mother's reassurance sounded smug and comfortless: " . . . But that means you have one son you don't have to worry about losing, isn't that so?"

Mr. Neale expressed embarrassment in rants and tirades. Chloë heard them all, through the screen door, the morning Don got the letter saying he wouldn't be called. "Failure and fairy, that's what F stands for!" boomed Mr. Neale, while his wife patted him and proffered pills he took for his heart condition, and Don nonchalantly dipped stiff rashers of bacon into pools of egg yolk. Catching sight of Chloë, he rose from the kitchen table, made a face at her, and closed the inner door. But she could still hear Mr. Neale shouting.

Now, in her own kitchen, Chloë is addressed by Don. "Your mother tells me you can read," he says, tapping a charred butt from the holder. "Anything good?" He raises his eyebrows and smiles expectantly.

With Jerry she is always sure: Jerry says what he means. Don is a puzzlement: she is wary of his tricks. "The funnies," she says, toying with the bear's plaid neck ribbon.

"The *funnies?*" Don hoots. "Mrs. Mack, how can you possibly let this brilliant child be content with reading the comics pages? Surely she's old enough for Horace and Virgil . . . "

"*You* were a prodigy, Donald," says Mother, defensive and embarrassed because she never wants to be caught doing something not socially correct.

"But Chloë is a prodigy, too, Mrs. Mack, really and truly." Don's face grows dark and serious, invisible hands reshaping his features. "You should think about enrolling her in the Lab School, you know. I really do mean that."

"We'll see," says Mother, irritated now and throwing beans into the pot with force instead of letting them gently drop.

Don changes the subject.

Jerry never came into the kitchen to talk to Mother. He never had the time. When he was home on leave he liked to visit his fiancée who lived in Evanston. *Really just a girlfriend*, Mrs. Neale said, cherishing her son's continued dependence. She and Mr. Neale had asked him not to marry while the war was on, she told Mother one day at the A&P, and he had agreed.

Jerry had been home several times since the Vincents' move to East End Avenue, wearing his smooth and spotless tan uniform with bars of colored ribbon on the jacket. Chloë liked his hat the best, a circle of tan cloth with a crisp bill. If he found Chloë sitting on her stool on the back landing he let her try it on.

Chloë saw Jerry nearly every day when he was home. She liked the Neale family best then. They seemed happier when all four of them were gathered around the kitchen table at breakfast. It was Jerry who made them lively, who told stories about people he had met in California, at the Marine base, and all the things he had seen on the train trips out and back. They were interesting stories, funny some of them, at least all the Neales laughed though often she didn't understand them, but she knew they were never mean or hurtful. Jerry never laughed at anybody. Don told stories, too, but they were jokes about people and their foolishness. Mrs. Neale, like Mother, delighted to hear him. Forced to share the breakfast table with his younger son, Mr. Neale said nothing and often rushed off to work without a second cup of coffee. With Jerry he lingered.

Jerry always talked to Chloë when he saw her, crouching down so that he could look directly in her eyes when he spoke, and she loved to be that close to him, admiring his firm, freshly shaved cheeks without Da's glaze of beard, his lingering lemon smell of after-shave. He would ask her about things she had done, trips to the park with Da and what she saw there, or shopping with Mother, and he always inquired after Ambrose. When she told him she could read *Dick Tracy* and *Mandrake the Magician* and *Smilin' Jack* on the comics pages he didn't laugh like Don. He said he liked them, too. For Ambrose he promised ribbon bars on his next trip home, and when Chloë said that pinning them into the bear's fur would hurt him, Jerry told her he would bring the bear a jacket, too.

She was wary of Don but attracted by him all the same. In a different way than Jerry, who was like some large warm animal she might lean against for comfort and protection. Don was thin and brittle, without sentiment, or so it seemed, but listening to him talk to Mother seemed an important thing to do, providing an oblique entry into realms of adult mystery.

Like her name, for instance, about which Chloë had puzzled but never asked: questioning Mother was hardly ever productive. But Don's queries, phrased as speculations, almost always drew responses.

Within weeks of the Vincents' moving in, Don had become a familiar presence at their own kitchen table in late afternoon, dropping in after classes for coffee and cigarettes while Mother prepared dinner. Mother began leaving the inner door open for him, a signal that she was at home and receiving visitors, though only Don ever called. One day, with Chloë in her accustomed corner perch, Don mused aloud about her name.

"So unusual," he said, speaking as though she were not in the room. "How did you come to call her Chloë, Mrs. Mack?"

Mother was ironing Da's shirts, pausing to sprinkle water on them from an old Coke bottle plugged with a perforated stopper. "Because of my brother Joe," said Mother, pressing a sleeve. "He was in the army in France during the first war."

"Yes?" said Don, peering at her over the edges of horn-rimmed glasses. He wore them on occasion. To make him look important, said Da. Perhaps older, said Mother.

Mother started on the next sleeve, not answering him.

"I mean, what would your brother's service in France have to do with it?" Don persisted.

Mother sat the iron on its heel and paused. "He had a girlfriend there. Her name was Chloë. He wrote us he was going to marry her but then he was shot and sent home." She resumed her ironing.

"You named your daughter after your brother's girlfriend?" Don sounded incredulous and, Chloë thought, rude. Mother seemed slightly embarrassed.

"I thought it was such a pretty name," she said, turning the shirt to iron the button placket. "I was just a little girl then, but he told me stories about France and it sounded so lovely . . . " She stopped for a moment and looked distant, as if searching for a memory. "So I wanted my own child to have a French girl's name."

"But it isn't French," said Don in what Da called his know-it-all way. "Certainly not originally. Chloë's the name of a girl in a famous story from ancient Greece. A novel, in fact. By a writer named Longus."

Mother blushed and looked flustered but kept on ironing. "The name means 'young verdure'—new greenery," Don said, smiling, pleased to impart knowledge.

"Is it a pleasant story?" Mother ventured.

"Oh, very much so!" Don beamed. "In fact, one of the pleasantest, you might say. With something in it for just about everyone." He smirked.

"But Chloë in the story—she's a good girl, I presume?" Mother looked concerned.

"Oh, absolutely," said Don.

"We didn't read Greek stories when I went to school," said Mother.

Chloë had heard about Joe before. Joe was only a partial secret, though she had no idea what he looked like; Mother had no pictures. Joe had been a mischievous child on the farm where they grew up, somewhere that Mother referred to only as Back East but might have been South, too. They had a Negro maid called Tillie, and that Joe, what a rascal, how he liked to tease her. Mother always laughed when she sat doing her sewing and talking about Joe. Talking to herself, it seemed, hardly noticing Chloë's presence, though sometimes she talked about Joe and Tillie when Don was in the kitchen. Mother's only memento of Joe was an ivory silk handkerchief, with American and French flags embroidered in blue and red silk. Joe had brought it back from France just for Mother. It lay on the bottom of her handkerchief box, wrapped in tissue, and was brought out for admiration from time to time. *Just think of it: all the way from France*, Mother would say. As if France were as far as the moon.

More secrets: The cigarettes Don smoked and the coffee he drank in such quantity in Mother's kitchen came from a man named Bundy. He was a friend of Da's who lived in Canada and once a month he traveled south by train to Chicago, bringing to Da's office at the downtown railroad station smoked meats and cheeses and Irish whiskey and honey and tins of coffee and cartons of cigarettes and sometimes even candies, nougats and rich cream-filled chocolates wrapped in gold and silver foil and little rectangles called torrone inside their own boxes with pictures of famous men, Italian kings and poets Da said, on top. "Heigh-ho, it's Bundy time!" Da would call out as he arrived in the kitchen, bringing the latest provender in two Goldblatt's shopping bags. Goldblatt's, a cheap department store in the Loop, had its own basement food market. Dad sometimes shopped there, and he saved the bags as camouflage for Bundy's goods. Bundy, it seemed, was a smuggler.

Food had been rationed for years, with the war going on. "We couldn't get by if it weren't for Bundy," Mother would say, helping Da lay out the latest delivery on the dining room table. The kitchen, adjacent to the back door landing, was deemed too risky: neighbors might appear. Though the secret source appeared to be safe with Don, who never asked but must have known where all the coffee and tobacco came from that he drank and smoked in Mother's kitchen. During the unpacking Chloë was allowed to sit on her knees on a chair and watch. This was much more interesting than the grocery store, with its tiresome waiting in line. Here Mother did not need her books of red and blue and brown and green ration stamps and her change purse of tokens to be exchanged for bits of tough meat and small packets of sugar and single sticks of butter and cans of drab vegetables. Here was ample food for royalty, and Da made its presentation into a regal ceremony, first removing and folding the crumpled newspapers stuffed on top of the brown shopping bags for added concealment, then drawing forth each package with deliberation and placing it carefully on the polished maple table for Mother's approbation. He might have been a prince, wooing her with jewels.

Once the trove had included a flat Planter's Peanuts can labeled with the company logo, a high-hatted, monocled peanut shell carrying a walking stick. Chloë hunched forward, putting her arms on the table to get a closer look. "Ah, someone wants Mr. Peanut," Da said, but Mother told him to wait till after dinner, the child's appetite would be spoiled. Chloë had writhed and squirmed throughout the meal that followed, thick slices of Bundy ham fried in bacon dripping. Mother had closed the windows so the neighbors couldn't smell. And then it was after-dinner at last, and Da reached for the Planter's can. Chloë watched with growing impatience as Da removed an attached small slotted key, slipped it into a small strip of metal on the side near the top, and slowly turned it, rolling the strip away from the can until it formed a tight disk and the lid was free. She licked her lips as Dad removed it and looked inside. Not peanuts but brown circles, lots of them, smelling of tobacco. "More cigarettes!" shrieked Mother, upending the can and tapping it carefully against the table. Several Camels slipped out. "Not my brand," said Mother, "but Don will be pleased." Chloë slid off the chair and went to her corner, seeking Ambrose for solace. No one noticed.

The war had been going on for a long time, from before Chloë could remember. Sometimes when it rained on Saturday Da took her to the movies over on Jeffrey Boulevard and there were always newsreels showing soldiers and sailors fighting far away. She could remember seeing real sailors when they lived by the lake, before they moved to South Shore. A navy training station was near the hotel, and when Da held her up to the window she could see men in white suits and caps marching on the pier. Sometimes, when she went to the Loop with Mother, she saw sailors and soldiers home on leave, walking along State Street. But Jerry was the only person she knew who was in the war.

He wasn't really fighting in the war, at least not yet. He was *stationed*, Mother said, at a base in California, where he did something in an office. He wanted to go to war, the real war, she knew; she heard the older Neales talking, arguing about it at the breakfast table. Jerry wanted to fight, and Mr. Neale said he should when the chance arose. Every time he said this Mrs. Neale would start to cry. She went to her neighborhood church nearly every day, St. Margaret's Episcopal, to pray that her son would be spared. Mr. Neale and the boys were Catholic. Mrs. Neale had refused to convert, as she told Mother proudly many times. Mrs. Neale was *socially a few cuts above* Mr. Neale, Mother had reported to Da, who was also an Episcopalian, though he never talked about it and only grunted when Mother said this. Mother herself was vague about her own religious background, letting it be known only that she was once a Presbyterian. Chloë had never been to church, though Da had taught her how to say her prayers.

The war was a state of being within which all things lived and moved, as basic and taken for granted as air and water and the trolley cars they rode around the Loop. Windows in their apartment were screened against the night by thick black window shades, *so the Germans and Japs can't see in*, Mother explained. Everyone made do with what they had; you couldn't buy much that was new, so nothing was thrown away: Coffee grounds and eggshells and bits of leftover food no one would eat were sprinkled on the Victory Garden that Da tended with neighbors in a vacant lot down the street. Bacon grease was saved in tins for reuse. Used bits of soap were hoarded, then pressed together to make new bars. Newspapers, along with rags not fit to clean or mend, joined bags of empty tin cans and toothpaste tubes and other metal scrap in the pantry closet. Every Saturday morning Da loaded them into Mother's shopping cart and wheeled it down the street to a place that collected such things for what Mother and Da called *the war effort*. From the radio, which Mother played all day long, came war news and war songs, and the newspapers—Da brought all of them home every day from work—blared stories and pictures of battle. Only a murder, or a fire, or an accident that killed and maimed, might take its place, and then only briefly. *War* was the first word Chloë learned to read.

The newsreels could be scary. Big silver planes roared across the screen, dropping bombs that whooshed down from the sky, hitting the ground with a terrible sound and spraying dirt, houses, trees, bodies, balls of flame and smoke into the air. And then the people who still lived, screaming, shouting, weeping into the camera, people she might have seen in better moods downtown, on State or Maxwell streets, women wearing babushkas and patched coats, men in dirty caps and overalls, sad-eyed children trembling in the rubble. That was Europe. What the narrator called The Pacific came next: more planes, more bombs exploding targets into bits. But here were ships firing large guns across the ocean, and houses of straw and wood, not stone and mortar, that burned away to nothing, and palms and vines blown into casual piles of debris. The people were different, too, with strangers' faces and pointed straw hats and layers of clothing wrapped around them, without buttons.

Sometimes Chloë saw the weekly newsreel twice, when she went to the movies in the same week with Mother as well as Da. Not together, of course: most of the movies she saw were *not really suitable for children*, that's what Mother and Da both said, frankly acknowledging a misdeed they were unable to resist committing. So when she went with Da on weekends she was told not to tell Mother, and when Mother took her to weekday matinees, she always said *Don't tell your father—he wouldn't approve.* Da liked Westerns and musicals, especially in color, though when movies for children were showing he took her to see these, too, and she was allowed to tell Mother she had gone. Mother never took her to children's pictures, preferring instead movies that featured women struggling with loneliness, or adultery, or poverty, or perhaps all three. At the movies Da bought her Black Crows but wiped the black stains from her mouth before they went home. With Mother she was allowed to share a small box of plain popcorn, no butter. Sometimes she fell asleep during Mother's pictures, which were nearly always in black-

and-white and more boring than scary. Though the newsreel often frightened her: when dead people came onscreen, hanging upside down from makeshift gallows or lying limp in rubble, she crawled under the seat until it was over.

Clothing was scarce, too, so Mother had to wear her old hats, of felt or straw according to season, touching them up with shoe polish. Sometimes she pinned artificial flowers or miniature bunches of fruit to their brims, choosing from a large collection she kept in a corset box in the closet. She added them to the necklines of her old dresses, too, trying to make them look different if not new. Da's suits were old, too, and Mother pressed and repressed them, running her iron over a damp towel she had placed on the wool to protect it from scorching.

Chloë's clothes were newer, some of them almost brand-new. They were hand-me-downs from Betty, the daughter of Da's boss at the train station. Betty had something wrong with her, though not like Dianne Click because Dianne's mind worked just fine, said Da. And not like earless Peter either, said Mother, who had met Betty once, before Chloë could remember, and said she looked like a normal little girl. Betty was retarded, said Mother, which meant slow; she lived at home and could never go to school. But her parents bought her lots of pretty clothes at Marshall Field's, which, said Mother, still had lots of clothing from before the war for those who were rich enough to afford it.

Every few months Da would come home from work with a green Marshall Field's shopping bag filled with Betty's neatly folded dresses and Mother would sort through them, deciding which Chloë might wear for everyday and which should be saved for what Mother called special occasions.

Mrs. Neale was always dressed up, perhaps because she went to church so often, and wore several diamond rings and a hat with a small veil. Unlike her younger son, Mrs. Neale was not inclined to back-porch visits. Mother encountered her on the street, in front of the building, or at the Jewel or A&P or Kroger's as they made their separate rounds from store to store in search of food. Chloë and Mother saw Mr. Neale, a burly man, at the drugstore from time to time, standing in a white coat behind the counter filling prescriptions, but he was the quiet type, said Mother, not given to conversation. With Chloë in tow, she met other neighbors shopping. The Gravys, Mr. and Mrs.—their real name was too long for everyday speech—had moved from Italy in the 1920s and owned a dry cleaning store on Jeffrey Boulevard, nor far from Mr. Neale's drugstore. They had a black-and-white dog called Jimmy, a long-haired spaniel who sat near the counter keeping an eye on customers. Jimmy lived at the store, apparently; she never saw him at home. She was told not to touch him.

The Morgans had a dog, too. He was named Duke and had white fluffy hair, and both Morgans said he was very old. Mrs. Morgan walked Duke three times a day, up and down the alley alongside their building. Duke let Chloë pet him and once, in winter, Mrs. Morgan let her take the leash. Duke urinated against a snowbank, melting it into a yellow crust, and then he sat down and refused to go any farther. Mrs. Morgan frowned and took back the leash.

Mrs. Morgan never smiled, and neither did her husband. His name was Henry, like the movie star, Mother said, though not related. Mr. Morgan was retired, said Mother, which meant he stayed home all day. He was also, said Mother, slightly peculiar, which was what Mother called people who did not respond when she spoke to them. Sometimes when Chloë went downstairs by herself to the Clicks' apartment she looked through the Morgans' screen door and saw Mr. Morgan at the kitchen table, staring out past her. When Chloë appeared he responded with rhymes, *Nosey, nosey, said Mrs. McPosey*, or *Mercy, mercy, said Mrs. McPhersey.* While he kept on staring.

Louisa, on the other hand, smiled all the time. Louisa was Dianne Click's day nursemaid, a fat Negro woman poured into a starched white uniform a size too small. She wore a stiff cap like a nurse's, held onto her head with bobbie pins. Dianne had rheumatic fever, said Mother, which meant she had a bad heart and couldn't run and play like other children. Dianne's parents worked all day, at the Board of Trade downtown, and Louisa took care of Dianne, pushing her in a wheelchair to the park when the weather was nice though she was older than Chloë and much too big not to walk. When it rained or was too cold to go out, Chloë might visit with Dianne at her apartment: Mrs. Click had said this to Mother, seeing her one day in the A&P not long after they moved.

Mother disapproved of Mrs. Click, who wore slacks and dyed her hair orange, and she did not encourage the friendship, though from time to time when she was feeling tired and out of sorts, Chloë was allowed to walk down two flights to the Clicks' and spend an hour or two with Dianne and her toys. Such visits were always occasions for anxiety: As she left, Chloë was admonished not to eat anything, nor was she to touch any combs or other personal items. Upon her return, she was made to scrub her hands twice with soap and hot water, and to change her clothes. Negroes, said Mother, had germs.

Despite Dianne's toys, a child-size stove and a sink with running water, curly-haired baby dolls in lacy silk garments trimmed in pink ribbon, a dollhouse with polished wood furniture and tiny china dishes and real electric lights, Chloë did not enjoy her visits. Dianne was whiny and didn't like to share, though Louisa tried to make her, and Chloë could only watch as Dianne ate cookies freshly baked by Louisa and drank chocolate milk. And then she had to wash up afterwards, and put on another dress. And she couldn't take Ambrose along. Again, because of the germs.

Dianne Click's grandmother came to see her sometimes on Sundays, and Dianne told Chloë she also had an aunt, and some cousins who went to high school. Where's your family, the rest of it, I mean, Dianne had asked Chloë one day. Chloë didn't know, and she told Mother about Dianne's question. "Back East," said Mother. "But not family like Dianne's, no aunts or grandparents. They're all gone." Gone where? Chloë wondered but didn't say, because Mother had firmed her lips and arranged the rest of her face into her no-more-conversation expression. "Gone where?" asked Dianne when Chloë told her the next time they met, and Chloë could only shrug. "You mean they're *dead*?" said Dianne. No no, said Chloë, they couldn't be dead, not like those broken people in newsreels, staring yet still and silent. Big, Chloë decided. Old, like the Morgans. Somewhere else, she said finally, and before Dianne could ask again it was time for Louisa's cookies and milk.

"Shoo, shoo, this whole building's Chloë's family," said Louisa, kindly and smiling. "Ev'rybody here be family, the human family's what they calls it."

"*You* aren't in my family," said Dianne, wrinkling her nose at Louisa. Who just smiled, and stroked the girl's hair.

Chloë did have an aunt, sort of. "Call me Aunt Lucille," Miss Snodgrass had said soon after their first meeting on the back stairwell, before Mother had time to object. Later Mother explained to her that a real aunt had to be Mother's or Father's sister, but it didn't matter to Chloë. Lucille Snodgrass was a bookkeeper who lived by herself, across from the Clicks. She had frizzled black hair, slicked with some sort of lotion smelling like flowers, and wore it pulled back in a bun. She gave Chloë books for Christmas and her birthday, Raggedy Ann stories that Mother kept on a high shelf and read to her only on special occasions.

And there were the Schneiders, across from the Morgans, refugees who had left Germany *just in time*, said Da, which meant before the war. Mr. Schneider took pictures for a living. His wife worked at Marshall Field's, cleaning floors and bathrooms. She had been a teacher *back home*, Da said, but her English was not so good. Mr. Schneider's wasn't much better, but no matter: his camera was his language. In his small studio he took pictures of brides and babies and servicemen and old people celebrating a long marriage. It was mostly *freude Arbeit*, happy work, he had told Da, who knew a little German and could translate. Though some of his soldiers had died, a great pity. Still, their mamas and papas had his photographs, as a way to remember. On her fourth birthday, in early spring, he had taken Chloë's picture in her best pink dress that had once been Betty's. Mother and Da had it on their dresser, in a golden frame Mother had bought on sale at Marshall Field's.

Was Mr. O'Connor family, too? He had no wife. Gone, said Mother. Away, thought Chloë. Surely she could not be dead: people only died in Europe, or The Pacific. Or perhaps Mr. O'Connor, who wore heavy brown dungarees with suspenders winter and summer alike, had left *her*. He was always working, shoveling coal and snow in winter, sweeping the sidewalk and mowing the grass in the front courtyard in summer. Once he had come to their kitchen to open the sink drain. He grunted instead of talking and never looked directly at you, and he always smelled of beer. So sad, said Mother, shaking her head with what seemed to be displeasure rather than sorrow.

The kitchen was where Mother had her accident, not long after Mr. O'Connor fixed the drain. Chloë was playing at the Clicks' when she heard Mother calling her name down the stairs. She came up and saw blood on the floor and Mother slumped in a chair with blood-smeared legs. "Get Louisa!" she ordered, "Mrs. Neale isn't home," and she ran back down and got Louisa, who told her to stay with Dianne while she went upstairs to help Mother. The Clicks had a phone, and Louisa called an ambulance. Then she called Da, who came home after Mother was driven off to the hospital. Which meant that he missed hearing her scream "NO MORE NO MORE NO MORE!" as the men carried her downstairs in a stretcher and Louisa hovered alongside her, stroking her arm and telling her to hush right up now, everything was going to be all right. Later, a week or maybe two, after Mother was home from the hospital, Dianne told Chloë that now she wouldn't have a baby sister or brother. "Not ever," said Dianne. But then Louisa told *her* to hush up and Chloë couldn't ask Dianne what she meant.

Late one night, when Chloë was supposed to be asleep but wasn't, she heard Mother say *no more no more no more* again, this time to Da. No more what, Chloë wondered, till she heard Mother's voice again. *No more brats. Ever. I can hardly cope with Chloë.* "Your mother made herself sick," Dianne whispered to Chloë a few days later at the Clicks', while Louisa was in the kitchen pouring milk. "That's what my mother says." Chloë wanted to know how, but Dianne couldn't or wouldn't tell.

That had been months ago, in the spring, sometime after Chloë's birthday. And now it was fall, and she no longer saw much of Dianne, who was taught at home because she couldn't go to school. The days tumbled on, one after another, the air growing colder, the sunlight thinner as she talked to Ambrose and shopped with Mother and went to the park with Da and the movies with each but not together and read the funnies. She had decided she liked *Smilin' Jack* the best because it had soldiers and stories about the war and reading it made her remember Jerry, even though Smilin' Jack Martin, who flew planes, was not in the Marines. There was also a man in the strip who only showed the back of his head because his face had been injured in the war, and another man, very fat, with a chicken walking beside him eating buttons as they popped off the man's tight suit.

Jerry had been home for the Fourth of July, when he promised a jacket and ribbons for Ambrose. When was he coming home again? she asked Da, but Da said no one could tell, only the President, a kindly looking man with a smile and a bowtie and thin grey hair whose picture was in the post office. So when Chloë went there with Mother to mail letters, she would stand in front of the picture while Mother bought stamps at the window and without speaking she would ask the man in the picture to send Jerry home soon. At night, after she had said *Now I lay me down to sleep* and asked God to bless Mother and Father, never Da because Mother was listening, she added Jerry's name, too. But she had greater faith in the man with the bowtie at the post office.

Hallowe'en came without celebration. Mother explained that it was a time when children got candy, but because of the war there wasn't much candy around, at least not enough to give away. And candy wasn't good for Chloë's teeth anyway, said Mother, while Da, sitting on the awning chair, hid his face behind a newspaper. They had a pheasant for Thanksgiving, from one of Da's other friends this time, fresh game not being one of Bundy's specialties, and Mother made stuffing from onions and stale bread. There was no cranberry sauce because a woman ahead of Mother in line at the Jewel had gotten the last can.

A week before Christmas Da brought home a small fir tree and wound lines of colored lights around its branches. Mother added foil icicles that she had saved, she said, since Christmas of 1936, when the King of England said he no longer wanted the job. She would hang them one by one, never in clumps as Da liked to do, and then stretch glittering strands of silky white hair across the branches. A few of the neighbors, the Clicks and the Gravys, put red plastic wreaths lit with electric candles in their windows, but Mother said they could not have any because the wreaths were cheap and in poor taste and besides came from Woolworth's.

And then it was Christmas Eve and Jerry was coming home. Mrs. Neale told all the neighbors, and nearly everyone in the building was down in the front lobby to meet him, even Duke, wearing a red bow. Only the Clicks weren't there; they had gone to Florida. When the taxi pulled up and he got out, they all cheered, even Mr. Morgan and Mr.

O'Connor, and they gathered around to shake his hand as he came inside.

Chloë reached out to touch his heavy woolen coat and felt melting flecks of snow. Seeing her now he knelt down and hugged her to him. "My dear little Chloë," he said softly, "I missed you." Then whispered into her ear "I didn't forget."

Christmas brought new mittens from Mother and a sled from Da and a big ham from Bundy for dinner. There were presents from neighbors, too: she was not allowed to have the jar of hard candy from the Schneiders, who didn't celebrate Christmas, and a blue blanket that Louisa made for Ambrose was discarded by Mother. But they kept the basket of oranges that the Clicks sent from Florida, and another book of stories of Raggedy Ann and Andy from Aunt Lucille, who didn't celebrate Christmas either, as well as pajamas for Chloë from Mrs. Morgan and an Italian cake from the Gravys, which Mother deemed fit to serve because it wasn't homemade. The Neales had a big red poinsettia delivered. Mr. O'Connor didn't give presents, Mother explained, because he worked for everyone in the building. Mother and Da gave him Bundy items, a wedge of cheese and a flask of Canadian Club.

Best of all was Jerry's jacket for Ambrose, just like his own but small, bear-size, which fit Ambrose snugly. "I mustn't feed him too much," Chloë confided to Da, thinking of the fat man in *Smilin' Jack* who lost his buttons. Jerry had not brought a hat, explaining that Ambrose's ears might get in the way. Chloë agreed. But there were colored ribbons, as he had promised, green, yellow, red, blue, and there were silver bars like Jerry's, too. Ambrose and Jerry were both first lieutenants.

At the post office three days later Chloë thanked the President on the wall.

Jerry was home for two weeks. It was cold, and the Neales kept their kitchen door closed, but Chloë played on the back porch in her snowsuit or sometimes in the courtyard and watched all the Neales come and go, Mrs. Neale to the grocery store and church, Mr. Neale to work, running up and down the stairs because he was always late. Don now had a part-time job at a bookstore in Hyde Park, so his visits to Mother's kitchen were shorter and less frequent. Jerry spent his days with Evelyn in Evanston.

Evelyn came to the Neales' apartment a few times, and then one day Chloë met her in the courtyard. She had long blond hair that curled under and blue eyes and a wide smile that showed shiny white teeth. She held out her hand so Chloë could see the ring Jerry had given her, a large diamond flanked on either side by clusters of small blue stones that she said were sapphires. It had been his grandmother's ring, Jerry said.

The ring made it true, thought Chloë. Now Jerry would marry Evelyn, that was what the ring meant. Her chin trembled, but she didn't cry till after Jerry and Evelyn had gone upstairs.

He was leaving on a Saturday afternoon. A taxi waited in front of the building to drive him to the train station downtown. It would take him nearly three whole days to get to California. And then he would board a ship, said Mother. The ship would take him to war in The Pacific.

Again, the neighbors came downstairs, this time to say goodbye. As before, they used their front doors, the ones that opened into carpeted halls and polished walnut staircases. But Chloë stood on the gray back porch holding on to Ambrose, refusing to go. Da had taken her stool inside.

"Naughty girl," Mother had said, pulling on her fancy shoes.

"After all the kindness he's shown you," said Da, looking disappointed.

But she wouldn't budge.

"We are going down now," said Da and Mother, closing the door in her face.

She stood there for minutes, hours, years, counting and recounting slats on the porch railing, watching their shadows move across the wooden floor in the fading sunlight.

And then someone was coming up the back stairs, climbing higher, higher.

"Chloë?"

He was there behind her, she knew that, wearing his cap and enormous brown shoes and the huge wool coat that smelled like smoke and wood, but she wouldn't turn around.

"I'd like to say goodbye to you, Chloë," he said gravely.

Chloë, still not turning, shook her head.

More steps on the stairs, familiar. Mother. Da.

"Kiss him, Chloë," said Da, reaching the landing.

"You won't see him for a long, long time. He's going to war." Mother, pushing ahead of Da to stand over her.

"Chloë, here, just take my hand," he said gently, but she couldn't, wouldn't turn around and let Mother see her cry.

He touched her cheek and kissed the top of her head. And after a moment started down the stairs.

"Naughty girl," said Mother and Da, following him down.

And then came the winter when people began to go away. Dogs first: Jimmy wasn't at the cleaners one day, and Mrs. Gravy told Mother he'd *passed*. He's gone, said Mother to Chloë, not explaining where. But then, days later, he was back, sitting in the window. He didn't move. "Mr. and Mrs. Gravy had him stuffed," said Mother, "so he can always be with them." His yellow-brown eyes were now made of glass and his hair was shiny, as though he'd been painted with nail polish. "You can touch him now," said Mother, but she didn't.

Duke went away with the Morgans. To Michigan, Mrs. Morgan told Mother the day the moving truck came. She and Mr. Morgan had a son there. They would live with him. Mr. and Mrs. Morgan were too old to climb stairs. They would write, Mrs. Morgan told Mother. They would send Christmas cards. A few days later new neighbors moved into the Morgans' apartment. They were teachers, said Mother, but she didn't know where. "They keep to themselves," said Mother, perhaps disapprovingly though it was hard to tell. "I don't think we'll be seeing much of them." Chloë tried to read their name on the doorbell downstairs, but she could only make out *Far--*. Mother and Da never called them by name. They became *the people in 3-A* and Don and Mrs. Neale called them that, too. "They don't mingle," said Mother.

And then one day Aunt Lucille told Mother she was moving to Denver, to be close to her brother. She invited Mother into her apartment and told Mother to help herself to anything that wasn't already packed in brown cardboard boxes for the movers. "But there was absolutely nothing there," Mother told Da later. "Not a stick of furniture—she'd sold it all. A few cracked cups in the kitchen. Some old magazines." And while Mother stood in the bedroom, Aunt Lucille had swept a small magnet across the floor, gathering a few stray pins. Jews were thrifty people, said Mother. A single man moved into Aunt Lucille's apartment. No one saw much of him, either, and Mother, who liked mystery, told Da that for all they knew 2-B was sheltering a man recently incarcerated. *Incarcerated* was a favorite word of Mother's. She would never have said *ex-con*. She seemed disappointed when Don told her 2-B worked for the gas company and went to St. Margaret's.

Mrs. Neale now went to church several times each day. Jerry was in The Pacific, she said, and she asked all the neighbors to pray for him, too. Mother told Da she thought that was tasteless. Religion, said Mother, was private and should not be discussed. "But she's worried sick," said Da, sitting in the awning chair and trying to read the newspaper. "Still," said Mother.

Chloë included Jerry in her prayers because Mother and Da told her to. But she didn't ask the President in the post office to bring Jerry home. When he came back he would marry Evelyn, he had told her so himself, and then he would go away and she would never ever see him again. She had already lost him; it was too late to bring him back.

One sock wouldn't go on. A thread was in the way, pushing back her little toe. The sock was pink, with tiny blue flowers on the cuff. Should she go into the kitchen and tell Mother, or get the scissors, forbidden to her, from Mother's dresser drawer? She started to open the drawer. *O my God!* she heard Mother shriek. She closed the drawer and ran to the kitchen, shoed and barefoot both.

Mother didn't notice her. Mother was standing at the door talking to someone. A man. 2B maybe, but no, it was Mr. Schneider in his winter coat with the brown fur collar. "Calm yourself," he was saying to Mother. He looked over her shoulder and glimpsed Chloë. "For the child's sake. You must calm yourself." He turned away and Mother closed the door.

Her face was screwed up in ugly red wrinkles. Was she angry or was she sad? Chloë couldn't tell.

"Where's your other shoe?" said Mother, and poured herself a cup of coffee. Da had gone to work. "Stupid, stupid, stupid," said Mother.

She looked at Chloë, who stood there, not moving. "She killed herself," said Mother. "All those sirens we heard, it was Mrs. Gravy."

"Sirens?" There were sirens all the time, up and down the boulevard that was only half a block away. Train whistles, too, from the South Shore Electric that ran alongside.

"Yes," said Mother, "sirens. *WhoooWhoooWhoo*," she mimicked. "You're a dreamer like your father, aren't you." She seemed annoyed. "How could anyone do such a thing? Climbs under a train and waits for the thing to move. Decapitated, he said." She turned to Chloë and a look of malicious pleasure stole across her face. "Do you know what that means? *De-CAP-uh-tat-ed*?"

Chloë shook her head.

"It means her head got chopped off."

She turned to the stove. "Let's see—did I feed you breakfast? . . . Must have. No more eggs in the pan.—Well, don't just stand there. Go find your other shoe." She sat down with her coffee and yesterday's *Herald-American*. Chloë retreated to the bedroom and pushed her foot into the sock until the thread broke.

The *Herald-American* that Da brought home from work had the whole story on page three.

"They found a butcher knife in her coat," said Da, handing the paper to Mother. "Just in case the train didn't finish her off—at least that's what the police said."

"Why on earth," said Mother, puffing on a Tareyton. She was stirring canned soup on the stove.

"The change, most likely." Da took off his coat and hung it on a peg by the back door.

"*Pah*," said Mother. "She must have been sixty at least."

Da shrugged and took over at the stove while Mother sat down to read the paper. She lit another cigarette.

Chloë said, "Maybe she was sad about Jimmy. Maybe she missed him."

Mother looked at Da and smiled slightly. "No one kills herself over a dog, silly."

"We'll have to find another cleaners," said Da. "Gravy's closing up shop."

"Those Japs, such awful people." Mother, ironing again.

"Japa*nese*, Mrs. Mack," Don corrected, recrossing his legs. He was dressed in his *Maroon* sweater, Mother called it, meaning something more than the color: he wore the sweater on days he worked at the college paper. He'd been laid off at the bookstore weeks earlier, after the holidays. "They're human beings, just like us. And the ones here, the Nisei, they're *Americans*, for pity's sake." He was smoking the last of the Planter's Camels.

"But think of the danger—they *have* to be incarcerated."

"That makes us no better than the Germans, putting them in concentration camps," Don protested.

Mother laughed at that and waved a hand dismissively. This conversation was getting too serious. It needed a nudge toward the frivolous; frivolity was what Mother ached for. "So tell me, Don," she said, choosing another of Da's shirts from the wicker laundry basket, "what's this about Elsa Maxwell getting *married?*" And she giggled like the girls Chloë saw at the movies, the ones who made such a fuss when the newsreels showed Frank Sinatra.

Mother didn't ask about Jerry and Don didn't tell.

Nothing had happened for days and weeks, nothing that Mother would have found exciting. No one, no thing, had left or changed since Mrs. Gravy's death. Mr. Gravy had closed the store and now lived alone in 2A, except for Jimmy; Da had seen him carrying the stuffed dog up the stairs one evening. Chloë still went to the Clicks once or twice a week, washing her hands and changing her clothes each time upon her return. She and Ambrose could not watch the breakfasting Neales; it was the off-season, too cold for open doors, but she always heard Mr. Neale rushing off to work, always late, running down the stairs six days a week, and she saw Mrs. Neale at the Jewel and the National and Kroger's and the A&P, and Don was in their kitchen almost every afternoon. Wednesdays were Joan-Crawford-Bette-Davis-dry-popcorn matinee-days with Mother, Saturdays and Sundays were Fred-Astaire-Bing-Crosby-Black-Crow-matinees with Da. Da still brought home sacks of limpa and pumpernickel from Goldblatt's and shopping bags crowned with newspaper that meant another Bundy delivery. Spring's arrival was noted, officially, though you wouldn't have known it: deep snow still banked the icy sidewalks.

Thinking about Jerry, which she did from time to time, especially when she dressed and undressed Ambrose, made her confused and sad and angry all at the same time, and she wondered if maybe Ambrose should not be wearing the ribboned jacket. But it felt like winter, and he would be cold: he had no other clothes. Evelyn had not reappeared. Mrs. Neale had told Mother at the butcher's that she hoped Jerry would reconsider, when he came home. Certainly a nice girl, Mrs. Neale had said. But for Jerry—well, Jerry was special and Jerry needed a very special wife. "He's too old for Chloë," Mother joked, and the child's face burned. Did that mean she still loved him after all?

The days, though, were changing, the length of them. Now it was light at six o'clock, the time Da got home. Spring was a week old the evening Da walked in the front door, most unusual, he had never done so before on a workday, startling Mother, who came out from the kitchen, followed by Chloë.

"What on earth," said Mother, drying her hands on a dish towel.

Da put down his big black briefcase, swollen with fat books about labor law. Before Christmas Da had told Mother he might change jobs again, maybe he'd be a lawyer, he'd always wanted to help the little guy. To which Mother had replied, *Over my dead body. You've got a good job and you're going to keep it.* But he still carried the books.

Tonight he said, "The child shouldn't hear this."

"You've been fired," said Mother accusingly and waved the dish towel at Chloë. "Shoo-shoo-shoo, child. Go in the bedroom. Your father and I have to talk."

Through the half-closed door she heard them. But it wasn't about losing his job. It wasn't even about them, their family. He'd met the Western Union boy in the courtyard. The boy had a telegram for Mr. and Mrs. Neale. He'd tried the bell, but no one answered. Where might he find them? The drugstore was still open. Da had told him to go there.

"Harriet's at church," said Mother.

"My God, I couldn't send him there," said Da.

"No, I don't suppose you could," said Mother, though she didn't sound all that sure.

At eight o'clock they put her to bed and said they were going out. Mother had on her fancy shoes and her best suit, with a wide lace collar.

"Where?" said Chloë.

"Just across the hall, if you must know," said Mother. "Now go to sleep."

She heard them leave through the living room, not the back door. They had left without hearing her say her prayers. To herself she now said *Now I lay me . . .* and then she blessed Mother and Da and Ambrose, and Mr. Gravy, who'd been included now that his wife was gone. Jerry: should she bless Jerry? Did he need her blessing? Did he need any single thing from her? Had he ever? She saw Evelyn's face, so pink, so beautiful with its perfect skin and eyes and halo of soft lovely hair. Mrs. Neale was wrong, she decided: Evelyn, she thought meanly, was too good for Jerry, not the other way round. She turned over in the cot and fell asleep.

The place, said Mother, was called *Ee-woe Jee-ma*. It was in The Pacific. There were lots of American soldiers there, fighting those wicked Japs. Jerry had been fighting with them. Jerry had been killed.

It was the next morning. Da had already left for work, extra early. Mother, it seems, was despatched to deliver the news to Chloë, after she ate her egg.

"And now," Mother said, "aren't you sorry you didn't say goodbye and kiss him? Your kiss might have made him live." She turned back to the black skillet she was scrubbing in the sink. "Just you remember that the next time."

The nightmares began a few days later. She didn't call them that then. They were bad dreams that woke her up in the night. Had she dreamed before this? She could not remember. But now, in sleep, she saw the dead, a man, a woman, sometimes children, once a parade of animals, floating lifeless downstream in a river, zebras, giraffes, a gorilla like Bushman at the Lincoln Park Zoo. They had been killed, all of them, *murdered*, and Chloë, yes Chloë, had done it.

"Nonsense," said Mother, annoyed to be awakened by Chloë's screaming. "You have no reason to cry," said Da. "Just be still, go back to sleep."

"I will spank you if you do this again," said Mother in the second week.

In the third week Chloë was spanked, hard, for five nights running.

In the fourth week Chloë learned to swallow her terror. The dreams still came, though not as often, and when they did she now held her hand over her mouth till she caught her breath.

Mrs. Neale has pictures, photographs. They're from Hawaii, Mrs. Neale tells Mother. Mrs. Neale has pressed the pictures into Mother's hands, "Here, see, this is where they put my boy," crying softly. She is standing at the front door. Mother has asked her in, though reluctantly, Chloë thinks, but Mrs. Neale shakes her head, no no, but I wanted you to see them, show them to Mr. Mack.

"Hawaii," says Mother, shutting the door. "I was there once, of course. Such a faraway place." She drops the pictures on the green desk blotter and goes back to the kitchen. Chloë picks up the pictures, five of them. White crosses, lots of white crosses, all lined up in some kind of field, a few of those pictures, from different angles, and two pictures of one of the crosses, one up close, one farther back. On the one up close you can see Jerry's name and some numbers.

"She brought over photos of Jerry's grave," says Mother to Da when he comes home that evening. "And why would she do that, pray tell?"

Da looks at them, one by one. "I guess she wants to share," says Da. "You sure can't tell it's Hawaii, can you." He drops them back on the desk and then notices Chloë sitting on the sofa with Ambrose. "Getting warm out," he says. "Time to take off that jacket, don't you think?"

The photographs of the cemetery and Jerry's grave remain on the desk for two days, a decent interval, Mother calls it, and then it's time, she says, to take them back to Mrs. Neale. That will be Chloë's job, Mother tells Da, because she herself cannot bear to do it, cannot bear the thought of having to watch Mrs. Neale break down all over again and cry copious tears. It's embarrassing, says Mother. Dad, reading the newspaper in his awning chair after breakfast on Saturday morning, says, "Of course."

Mother hands the pictures to Chloë. "You are to go across the hall and give these to Mrs. Neale, understand?"

The front door clicks behind Chloë, who wonders—briefly, terrifyingly—if she will be able to get back inside afterward. She wishes she had brought Ambrose for comfort.

Mrs. Neale answers Chloë's knock.

"Oh, you precious thing!" gushes Mrs. Neale, bending down to hug her. Mrs. Neale's face is soft with powder that smells like flowers. She pulls Chloë inside and closes the door.

"So you've brought me my pictures," she says, not unkindly, taking them from Chloë's outstretched hand. Mrs. Neale wears rings, silver-colored bands with lots of winking diamonds, on both of her bony hands. She moves over to a large sofa and gestures for Chloë to sit beside her. The sofa is dark blue, the same blue as the ropy veins that bulge through the taut skin of Mrs. Neale's hands.

"I miss him so much," says Mrs. Neale, spreading the pictures in her lap. From a pocket in her grey silk dress she produces a lacy white handkerchief and dabs at her eyes. Chloë, perched on the sofa, wonders if she should apologize now, or wait for Mrs. Neale to speak.

"And you do, too," says Mrs. Neale, giving Chloë another hug.

The hugs must mean that Mrs. Neale doesn't know.

"They're bringing him back, of course," says Mrs. Neale, rearranging the pictures. "After this awful war is over, they're bringing him back. To Arlington."

Where and what is Arlington?

"My mother has been to Hawaii," says Chloë, pulling at her dress. It is too short.

"And then Mr. Neale and I will go there, with Don of course. It will be a special funeral, a special time." She starts to cry again and her knees shake and the pictures tumble to the carpet.

Chloë puts her right hand on Mrs. Neale's knee. "I'm sorry," she says.

Mrs. Neale bends over to gather the pictures. "I know you are, honey, I know you are. He really loved you, you know that."

"He loved Evelyn," says Chloë, feeling bolder, willing to risk. Wishing to be contradicted.

Which Mrs. Neale does, sort of:

"And now no grandchildren. None." Mrs. Neale frowns.

But I could be your grandchild, I could live in Jerry's room and go with Don every day to campus, to the Lab School. And maybe help Mr. Neale in the pharmacy when I got older. I could be useful, I would be quiet, I would cause no trouble.

But no, that would not happen, would it. Because they would find out, wouldn't they.

Mother would tell.

"Life is terribly cruel," says Mrs. Neale. But her tears are gone. She gets up, clutching the pictures in one hand and easing Chloë off the sofa with the other, guiding her toward the door.

"You be a good girl now, you hear?"

And then the phone is ringing and Mrs. Neale without saying goodbye opens the door and closes it behind Chloë and goes on with her own life. As does Chloë, though she will wonder forever if a simple kiss might have changed the world.

Where You Are

Our mother isn't here. . . .

I've heard it many times, that little girl's voice, high-pitched, plaintive. A little blond girl, six, nearly seven the paper said. *Unkempt:* that's what *my* mother would say. Would have said: *Such an* unkempt *little girl. Stringy hair, unwashed since God knows when, and her clothes! Stained with Pop-Tarts and Kool-Aid and all the other junk her mother feeds her and that dim-witted brother.*

The brother. Looked to be about four. I don't remember him, do I? Saying anything, I mean. But: he can't speak. Or won't. Couldn't and wouldn't. Running along by her side, hitching up too-big jeans, snot-nosed, mud-crusted. Did he ever wear shoes? His feet must have hurt, running on that gravel road.

Our mother isn't here. . . .

I saw Mother's picture today. In my mind's eye, I mean. I need no real pictures of Mother around. Capital M Mother. The memories suffice. Her navy-blue back and those smart two-toned pumps, spectators they were called, striking the pavement like crisp matches. The back receding with the match sounds, melding into the crowd. Running toward her. But not *her*. Another plumpish woman in navy-blue with a dark-feathered hat who says she is not my mother, *but maybe we can find her, dear*. And we rush ahead, she pulling me, pushing through hard-boned people until we are right up behind Mother. *Here she is, the naughty girl,* says the feather-hat woman, tapping Mother on the shoulder without breaking stride, and the three of us make a sudden stationary knot in that mass of moving people as Mother stops and turns and says *Naughty indeed! And here I thought she was right beside me the whole time . . .*

Which of course is not true. She left me in the five-and-ten, playing with the metal wind-up bugs that the saleslady said came from Japan. *See*, she said, turning over an enameled cricket and pointing knowingly to the name stamped on the back. *Prewar. It doesn't say Occupied.* The fronts were painted shiny yellow and green with black dots and lines for eyes and wings. *Japan!* said Mother with annoyance. *We're not buying anything made by Japs.* And then she said she was going over to see the knife man do his demonstration. The knife man sold bread knives and meat cleavers and can openers with corkscrews attached, but sometimes he was the toaster man or the Mixmaster man. That day it was toasters, and I lingered with the bugs as I watched Mother walk with clear intent down the center aisle, never giving an eye to the toasters, past the cash register right out the front door and into the moving crowd. Never looked back. Naturally I dropped the bug I was holding and started to follow but the saleslady thought I still had the bug, so that kept me back a few minutes. When I got out the door and turned right, as Mother had done, I thought I saw her way up ahead, almost to the next block. But, as I said, it was the feather-hat lady.

Mother was disappointed, of course, to be found. She ran off for good a few weeks later, during a Mixmaster demonstration. The saleslady in toys called the police. The policeman who came was nice; he even bought me a bug but said I had to promise to watch out for the sharp edges. He said they didn't make things well in Japan. One of his own kids had been cut on the hand by a Jap toy. But since I was crying, he said, he'd let me have one. But I had to promise.

The little girl's name was Claudia. I can't remember her brother's name. The mother was Muriel, I remember that. Sometimes I'd get her mail: *Mrs. Muriel Mutzenbrenner.* No, not really, but something unpronounceable, with lots of harsh consonants. Kids at school must have laughed at Claudia, with a name like that. Was Muriel truly a Mrs.? There was no sign of Mr. M. A grandmother, some older woman Claudia called Mamaw, lived in a little shed out back, an old chicken coop.

White trash. Mother again. A Mamaw lived above us on 53rd Street. Up from Kentucky, Mother said. Cleaned toilets at Marshall Field's. *They test them there. Give people jobs they can handle. So you see, that Mamaw woman is pretty far down.* Always the tripartite mantra: *Don't stare, don't speak, do not engage in conversation.* I was Claudia's age then, or thereabouts. Claudia never talked to strangers either. Except me. But I wasn't really a stranger, was I?

Our mother isn't here . . .

Well, it's like this: he'd left me, *my* Mr. M, I'll call him, though his name came easier off the tongue than Muriel's, and I had to find something cheap. We'd been renting month to month, a place down near the Flatiron before the district got fixed up, but the rent was too high for me alone. I worked a few blocks away but the job wasn't much. I could get by almost anywhere with the skills I had. All I needed was a cheap place to live. Then I saw an ad in the company newsletter for a small country house, and by small I mean four rooms. And don't be misled by "country house." This was your basic rustic cottage, nearly two hours north, off the Thruway. The owner wanted someone to keep an eye on the place. Perfect for a person like yourself, he said, when I went upstairs to Personnel to see him. If I move there I can't work here anymore, I said, explaining the obvious. Suit yourself, he said. They'd have no trouble filling my job. With vacation pay, he figured I'd have enough to make the monthly rent.

So I moved the cat and two suitcases of clothing and ten boxes of books and the Eames chair that my Mr. M, in a passing spurt of generosity, had bought as a birthday present for himself and then left behind.

I arrived in a rented pickup on June 20. The first day of summer. It had been a dry spring, and the fat wheels kicked up a small sirocco on the gravel road leading up to the Cheetham place. That's what it was called by the people down at the market, where they also pumped gas and held the mail. You be needing yourself a car? they wanted to know when I went down to pick up milk and cat food on the first afternoon. Because somebody's cousin had a Ford they could sell me, real cheap.

I have a bike, I said.

Train station's ten miles off, they said. You fixin' to ride all that way every time you go inna city? 'Cause somebody has a brother what could drive you over there any time you wanted. Don't want to go, I said. Not now.

I stayed the first night at the policeman's house. The boy who'd cut his hand on the wind-up bug was about my age, and he taught me how to play checkers. The house smelled of food cooking, the kind of smell that Mother always complained about when she sniffed the air in our apartment. Always Mamaw, or at least that's who Mother blamed, cooking something for herself and her son, who couldn't work and wore an oxygen tank strapped to his back. I liked the smell: it was warm and friendly and human, and meant that people cared for each other. But the policeman's son couldn't read very well, and I had to help him sound out the words in his Superman comic books. The policeman's wife said I was very smart for my age, and wasn't it a shame, and their apartment looked big enough to me. Big enough for me to stay. But the next day I was taken to the orphanage. Only till we find your mother, they told me, but I stayed till I was sixteen.

When I ran away they didn't come looking, or if they did they didn't find me.

And sixteen years after that, the details of which are irrelevant to this story, I was living at, or on, the Cheetham place. The first morning, I saw Claudia and her brother standing across the road, looking in my direction. I wheeled the bike out from around back and pushed it down the cinder driveway. Dry as a bone, and Claudia wore scuffed yellow rain boots. Holding on tight to her brother's hand, pulling him toward me.

I have to confess I'm not fond of small children. Mr. M wasn't either. You might say that's what brought us together. Then somewhere along the way he changed his mind, or so he said; at any rate, when he left, he moved uptown to await the birth of his first child. A fling at work had turned into something more serious, apparently.

On that morning in the country I felt the need to be nice, despite six years of hearing Mother warn against the dangers of poor whites. I knew about Claudia, and her brother and her mother, from the owner, the man in Personnel, who said they stayed to themselves and wouldn't be a bother. They were tenants, too, as were the Negro family with nine children who lived half a mile up the road. Mother had never said a word about Negroes, there having been none nearby to be cautioned against, but the opportunity for conversation never arose with this Negro family: they *kept their own company*, the same as Mother and Father said *they* did way back when.

But as I said, on that June morning I felt the necessity for kindness toward these two children, so I chatted politely for a moment, then went back inside and brought out a children's book, lots of pictures, something classic. For you, I said, handing it to Claudia. And your brother. You can read it to him.

And after that I was Claudia's best friend. She was always standing in the road with her brother, watching my house, waiting for me. The brother never said a thing, just stared and chewed on his forefinger. Over the following months I gave Claudia half a dozen books; leftovers from Mr. M, who worked for a time in publishing. Sometimes her brother would reach over with his free hand and touch the cover, as if trying to prove to himself it was real.

I think Father may have left because of Mamaw's cooking, though I couldn't say for sure. I don't ever remember hearing Father and Mother quarrel, though occasionally she would express exasperation, as for instance on the evening he came home with a live duck. The duck, quacking furiously, was riding under his arm in a brown cardboard liquor box. A liquor bottle, I don't remember if it was the same brand, was in his other hand. Father took the duck out of the box and put it in the bathtub with a few inches of water. Mother said it would fly away. Father said it was not that kind of duck. Mother said she would like to bathe, and now how could she? Father suggested she get in the tub with the duck. Then he poured himself a drink from the bottle into a toothbrush glass and leaned against the bathroom sink and upended the glass into his mouth. I was watching in the doorway. Some of the whiskey spilled down his face. Mother said this was the final straw, and she didn't have to put up with such behavior. Father sniffed the air. Mamaw's cooking odors were coming through the exhaust vent in the wall. Neither do I, said Father. You can't even cook a man a decent meal.

Well, I'm leaving, said Mother. Oh, no, said Father. Me first. And out he went. I never saw him again. Mother called the janitor, who seemed happy to get the duck.

I got a job a few miles away, at a small printing plant that published the weekly newspaper and a local almanac and various forms, receipt books and such, for farmers and local businessmen. It was the right sort of mind-numbing work, proofreading tractor ads and notices of grange meetings and church suppers while I decided what I wanted to do with the rest of my life. I had a steady routine all those months in the country. Work six days a week, home on the seventh, reading my way through the Sunday *Times* that I biked to the market at 8 a.m. sharp to buy. And day in and day out, Claudia and her brother out in front by the side of the road. Watching. In the background glimpses of Muriel their mother, hanging up clothes, feeding chickens they kept out back, swinging an axe over piles of empty cans she flattened for the scavenger. The man in Personnel said she had a job someplace, he wasn't sure where. The unseen Mamaw was supposed to be watching the kids.

In early September they went to school, Claudia and her brother both, though he seemed too young, riding away on the big yellow bus that drove up the road and back every weekday morning and riding back on the same bus in late afternoon. Though I imagined the return trip, because of course I was at work when they came home. So now I saw the two of them only on Saturday mornings when I'd bike off to work, and sometimes on Sunday afternoons, after they'd been in church for hours, and I'd go outside to clean up some of the leaves that were starting to fall. Claudia liked to sing, she told me; that was the best part about the church they went to. Would I like to hear one of the songs? She chanted the same words over and over again,

Brighten the corner where you are!
Shine for Jesus where you are!

tunelessly repeating herself, while the mute, stolid brother, finger in mouth, methodically moved his foot up and down to the beat.

I had to come home from work around noon one day in early November to let in a repairman, someone the man from Personnel had hired. Was it the furnace, maybe, or the water pump? I can't remember, though I do recall it was cold, too cold to ride the bike anymore so I was walking the two miles back and forth to the printing plant. Country life seemed desolate now that the trees were leafless, and the sky was no longer blue but a cloudy grey, and thick patches of grass and weeds had turned a dull brown. Lasting out the winter seemed a glum prospect; on the other hand I had nowhere else to go.

The repairman was sitting in his pickup in the cinder driveway. A country song played on the truck radio, something about beer and sorrow and fickle women. The air was so still the song might have carried far into the next county.

He was grizzled but probably not much older than forty. Country living ages people, apparently. He fixed whatever it was that was broken without saying much, only asking once for a glass of water before he packed up his tools to leave.

You know them folks across the way? He jerked his head toward Claudia's house. *Them's my kids.* He cleared his throat and shot brownish spittle out the door. *But SHE don't let me see 'em.*

Did I say they were nice children? I don't remember. I just wanted him to go, and at that moment I wanted to get away myself, far away in another direction.

I tried looking for Father and Mother once. It was before my Mr. M, who never knew about Mother and Father disappearing or anything at all about my early life. He was not a curious person. They were polite, the people back at the orphanage when I called, but said they couldn't give out any information without a judge's order and did I have an order from a judge and since I did not they could not help. I called the police department, and social welfare, but they both said it was too long ago, records were lost, didn't I know about that big fire a few years back, and no, they could not help me. Mother was from somewhere in the East, I believe; at least that's what she said, though my birth certificate, under Mother's Place of Birth, says Topeka. As for Father, I really couldn't say. Their names were common ones. I could be related to almost anyone in the country.

The day before Thanksgiving I came back to the house early in the afternoon to pack a small bag of clothes and leave extra food for the cat. A friend, someone I knew from my old job, had invited me for dinner in the city, and after months of country living I was ready to be there again, at least for a few days. It was starting to snow lightly when I locked up the house and started down the driveway, en route to the market a mile away. The brother what had the car was going to drive me to the train.

And then as I reach the road here comes Claudia, running running down the sloping front yard of her house, running toward me, into me, clutching at my baggy duffle coat. *Our mother isn't here . . . please, please . . .* But what is she asking me to do? I have somewhere to go, I can't stop for this dirty child, wearing no coat over her thin dress, only socks on her feet. *Our mother isn't here!* Insistently she cries this over and over, attaching herself to the suitcase so that she is dragged down the road until I finally break free and walk, run from her, toward the highway and the market and another life. I can't, I can't, I tell her. I can't stop. I have someplace to go, I'm late, I'll miss my train. Go take care of your brother. *But our mother isn't here!*

Did she tell me about her brother then? I don't remember. I hurried on down the road and reached the highway, then looked around and saw her running back up toward the house, screaming bloody murder.

Which is what it was. The father, apparently. The Thanksgiving Eve Murders. It was in all the papers. Section B of the *Times.* I read about it the next day, in the evening, after dinner. My hostess had told me that morning, of course; she heard it on the news. Didn't I live in the same county? Don't know those people, I said; *of course* I didn't know such people.

Claudia survived, even though her wounds were severe, according to the papers; there was a follow-up story six months later. Her father turned the hatchet on himself, hard to imagine but true, after killing his son, and the invisible Mamaw, too, so there's nobody left to pay the price of the crime except Claudia. I suppose it was the same hatchet Muriel used to flatten the cans, *thwack thwack thwack,* behind the chicken house. Muriel disappeared. Claudia went to a foster home. I moved back to the city in December after the furnace gave out. I got my old job back, and I found a cheap room on the Upper West Side. Sometimes when I walked home from work I'd see my Mr. M up ahead pushing his child in a stroller. A girl. I'd cross the street just to avoid having to exchange pleasantries, but it didn't bother me to see him. Not really.

That was a long time ago. I'm twice the age I was when Mr. M had his little fling. Twice the age I was when I lived across the road from Claudia. I still think about her now and then. At first, after I moved back to the city, I considered looking her up. But what could I offer? I have no home. I couldn't keep a young girl who was probably half nuts after what she'd been through. But I still hear her voice sometimes. *Our mother isn't here . . .*

What if I'd stopped, back there in the road? What if I'd taken her in my arms and said right then and there, *You're coming with me, just come, no questions.*

Was I wrong not to?

Parallel Lives

The nurse was older and kindly, older meaning she was grey-haired and matronly and therefore over forty; kindly meant gentle, considerate, not like her mother.

Well, imagine that, her mother was saying in the accent she used in public. Both of us from Georgia, both of us a long way from home. The nurse nodded and smiled slightly; she was taking Sarah's blood pressure.

Sarah was seventeen. She was in the hospital to have surgery. Something serious, something to do with whether or not she could ever have children. "Of course," her mother had said in the doctor's office, "not having children isn't necessarily a bad thing, now is it?" Meaning she didn't want to pay for the operation. The doctor disagreed.

Sarah had finished high school a few weeks ago. Nearly top of her class, only surpassed by a boy headed to Harvard in the fall. She was also going east, that is if she came out of the surgery. A woman's college on full scholarship. Her mother hadn't liked the idea. The college counselor, the school principal, her French and math and history teachers, all of them disagreed with her mother.

Her mother had left the room. Mrs. B, the nurse, leaned over and whispered, "You'll be okay, you hear? Everything will be just fine." She smelled of starch and rose perfume and disinfectant. An agreeable, reassuring smell.

Mrs. B was a widow, like her own mother. Except it hadn't made Mrs. B bitter or brittle or whatever word defined her mother's unhappiness. Some people could transform their sorrow into gifts of empathy. This, she sensed, was what Mrs. B did. But others, like her mother, made sorrow a weapon, assaulting the world with their misery. Slyly, deviously: rather than full-throttle assaults, her mother picked and poked and twisted, enacting elaborate maneuvers of subtle torture. Widowhood, Sarah suspected, had little to do with it, though it couldn't have helped. Her mother, she thought, had been born that way. Sarah barely remembered her father; he had died in a car crash when she was three. Sometimes, seeing her mother at her worst, Sarah wondered if his death had really been accidental.

Sarah learned about Mrs. B in the recovery room, about her widowhood, about her life as a nurse. About the hospital in Washington, DC, where she'd trained before the war. About her daughter. Mrs. B also had a Sarah, spelled *Sara*, no *h*. Mrs. B sat by her bedside, holding her hand, drawing her back to consciousness, speaking of family, summer, college, future. Daylight peeked through the slanted blinds. Machines pumped and sloshed. An old woman in the next bed dozed, or maybe she was dead and no one had noticed. Sarah tried to speak but sleep still claimed her, denied her words. Mrs. B was talking about her own daughter, *just your age, imagine that. But going west to school, not east. Maybe someday you'll meet her. You'd like her, she'd like you, I'm sure of it. . . . There now, I know, dear, I know it hurts, we'll get you something, just wait, we'll make it better . . .*

Which she did. Sarah was in the hospital for nearly three weeks and every day she was there Mrs. B did something for her. Played Scrabble, brought her home-baked cookies and dusting powder and Agatha Christie mysteries—*yes, I know she's light but that's what you need right now, no heavy reading till you're feeling tiptop, my girl!* And of course she was right; Agatha Christie was just the thing. And on her day off there was Sunday television, *Omnibus* and the like, quietly provided by Mrs. B. Her mother had called it a frivolous expense and refused to pay.

On the day Sarah checked out, she hugged Mrs. B and cried. She promised to write, and did, a few times anyway. The last was a note from college. *I hope you are well,* she had written, *and I hope your Sara is enjoying herself and that you are not too lonely in her absence.* And then, before signing her name, instead of saying *Sincerely* or *Cordially* or *Very truly yours*, conventions of correspondence etiquette learned from her mother, Sarah had written *I love you and will never forget you.*

But she did, of course. Mrs. B dropped out of everyday consciousness. Sarah stayed in the east after college, after her mother died. Both events occurred in quick succession, her mother's death first. It was, like her father's, also said to have been an accident. If you could call falling off a train platform accidental. Although Sarah supposed it happened, sometimes.

Sarah did not fulfill her early promise. It was too hard then, for women, or so it seemed. Professors, all female, encouraged her to go to graduate school, be an academic. Sarah didn't want to be just like them, alone or living with other women and looking like Eleanor Roosevelt. Sarah wanted a family of her own. She moved to New York, went to Katie Gibbs like most of her classmates, and got a job as a secretary at Prudential. She lived at the Barbizon with other overeducated young secretaries and rode the bus downtown and back every day. Like most of her classmates and the other women her own age who lived at the Barbizon, she was married within a year.

She thought about Mrs. B again when she went to the doctor two weeks before the wedding, to get a diaphragm. She wasn't sure she needed it, she told the doctor. Six years earlier she had had surgery, she said, and it might not have worked. Time will tell, the doctor said, but meanwhile you should give this a try. Get used to marriage first, before you have a child.

The surgery *had* worked, apparently. Two years later, ready to start a family, she became pregnant the first time she left the diaphragm—*the appliance,* her prissy husband called it—in the bathroom cabinet. She delivered a girl nine months later. When her daughter was two she conceived a son in spite of the diaphragm and generous dollops of Ortho-Crème.

They moved to the suburbs, and Sarah joined the League of Women Voters and the PTA, and drove her daughter to ballet class and her son to Little League. Her husband, a stockbroker, had two affairs, one with his secretary, a young woman who had gone to Sarah's own college and then to Katie Gibbs, the second—after his secretary left for a higher-paying job and a more promising, unmarried and childless boss—with the wife of his best friend, a woman Sarah knew only because they worked together at the annual school carnival. The woman played golf and tennis and bridge, and Sarah, who was not athletic, detested card games, and preferred to read in her spare time, did not like her. Neither, ultimately, did the woman's husband, who divorced her on grounds of adultery. Richard, Sarah's husband, could not decide whether or not he wanted to marry his former best friend's former wife, whose name was Cecily. He asked Sarah what she thought he should do. Sarah, rallying herself for a final assault on the stupefying boredom of married life, said, "Go for it!" with a gusto that surprised her. Richard, pleased that a decision had been made for him, obliged. Sarah, also claiming adultery, collected a handsome sum in court. Enough to start life over again. For years she treasured her last glimpse of Richard and Cecily, and Cecily's three children (one of whom was autistic), and Richard and Sarah's son and daughter, standing in the driveway of the Scarsdale colonial, looking dumbfounded. "They're yours," she had told Richard and Cecily before driving off. "In a few years' time maybe they can come see me. On visits. After I'm settled."

She regretted, a tiny bit, leaving the children behind. But they were better off, she told herself. Eleven years with Richard had taught her she wasn't meant to be a wife or mother.

Sarah moved to a university town in the Midwest. She picked it out at random on a Rand McNally U.S. atlas, a moving-in present from the State Farm agent in Scarsdale. His name and address and phone number were rubber-stamped on the front cover in black ink. She had written her former name, her married name, underneath. The town was neither big nor small, about thirty thousand. She arrived a few days ahead of the movers, rented an old frame cottage a few blocks from campus, and spent six weeks arranging her furniture, hanging pictures, shelving books, cutting grass. Then, on a Tuesday afternoon in late September, she walked to the university library and asked for a job. She could type, she said, and file, and had a degree from Wellesley, which they said they'd never heard of but hired her anyway.

On her first day at work, the following Monday, she was assigned to the catalogue room and handed a stack of Slavics journals. She had listed Russian proficiency on her résumé. "I'm impressed," said a young woman sitting across from her, after they were introduced. "I only know

French, and that's pretty useless these days." The woman, also called Sarah, had a nice smile, Sarah thought, but said nothing further the rest of the morning.

"How will they tell us apart?" Sarah ventured to ask over lunch. They had both brought sandwiches from home and ate at their desks.

"That's easy enough. You're Sarah with an *h,* aren't you? So you can be *Sarah H.* I'm without, so I'll be Sara *B. B* for my surname, maiden name that is." And told Sarah what it was.

"Did you grow up in Chicago?" Sarah asked. "And was your mother a nurse?"

As it happened, Sara B had led a not dissimilar life, though she'd gone west for college, to Mills in Oakland. No Katie Gibbs, either; she'd married a graduate student at Berkeley after graduation. And no suburbs. They moved to Washington State, where he taught and finished his dissertation. Sara B worked as a secretary in her husband's department. Then she had two daughters, thirteen months apart. A few years later, her husband was offered a tenure-track position here, at the local university. So she packed up their little household and drove the trailer, and herself and the children and Stanley, her husband, who couldn't and wouldn't drive, to their new home, a house her mother's savings had bought them south of town. That had been six years ago. Only she wasn't living there, or with Stanley and the children, anymore.

Four years ago, during the summer term, her mother had suddenly become ill, advanced uterine cancer. Sara went up to Chicago to see her, leaving the children with Stanley, who was not teaching over the summer and had no other responsibilities. On the fourth day, she received a call from the local police; they'd gotten her mother's number from Stanley. He was in jail at the county courthouse. The police were asking if she would post bail. Stanley was pretty distraught, they said, though later she was not sure that *distraught* was the word they used; they probably said *upset*, more likely in a small town. Stanley was being charged with negligent homicide. The children were dead, killed in a fire that also destroyed the house. Stanley had left them alone so he could fuck the blonde assistant professor of psychology who lived down the street. The police did not use the word *fuck* but Sara understood what they meant. He'd only been gone a few minutes, he'd swear to it, Stanley told her when they put him on the phone. Sara said no and hung up. Her mother died a week later.

Sara B lived in the same neighborhood as Sara*h*. Three streets away. She came over for dinner the same evening, bringing a bottle of Almadén and half a pound cake she'd baked the day before. Not for a lover, she said; the other half had gone to a math professor's widow who lived next door. She was no longer interested in men, or having a family, she said, not after Stanley. Who'd been sent to prison for several years, then released for good behavior. He'd gone back to the West Coast. Would you believe it, Sara B said, he was hired at Berkeley. It's the sixties, remember, said Sara*h*, and Sara B nodded in a knowing way.

"It's like we're sisters," said Sara B. She was sitting on the floor of Sara*h*'s living room, teaching herself macramé. Sara*h*, hunched in her bentwood rocker, worked on a crossword. A recently acquired cat, Siamese, dozed in her lap.

"Yes," said Sara*h*. "I think we are."

In the spring Sara*h* gave up her lease and moved her books and her furniture and her pictures to Sara B's place, which was bigger. They bought a second cat. They went to concerts at the music school, shopped together at Kroger's (which had lower prices than the A&P), and bought a piano so they could play Schubert duets. During the winter they read aloud to each other every evening, after dinner. Whoever cooked was the listener. They began with *Portrait of a Lady*, which both of them had read before, of course, years ago. Now both confessed they found Isabel Archer, this time around, a fool. "Though you have to remember: this was 1870," Sara B reminded. "And therefore make allowances," Sara*h* agreed. They read more James, all of Dickens, every Shakespeare play except *Titus Andronicus* (they thought it was silly), some of Conrad and Hardy, and then the continental Europeans, Dostoyevsky, Tolstoy, Mann, and all the rest. All the rest worth reading, as Sara*h* put it.

After forty years they still had more to go. Asians, they decided, Lady Murasaki and the like, would be held in reserve for old *old* age.

They continued at the library, Sara B with her French catalogue, Sara*h* with her Russians. They had two weeks' vacation, at first, each year; then three and eventually four. Early on they went to Europe one summer, the trip they should have taken after college but did not. And ten years later they drove to Canada, Banff, and stayed at Lake Louise because Sara B had always wanted to visit the place where her parents honeymooned. She had their picture on the living room wall, a black-and-white photo of a smiling couple, arm in arm, standing in front of the famous chateau. After that, Sara B and Sara*h* stayed home. There were no relatives to visit, neither nearby nor in far-off places. Early on, Sara*h* wondered from time to time about her children, but she never heard from them, or from Richard.

They had acquaintances, other people who worked in the library, neighbors, a man who cut the grass and put up the storm windows when they decided they could no longer do these things themselves. But no friends other than themselves.

They are sitting in the living room, Sara B and Sara*h*, reading the Sunday *Times*. They can have it delivered now; the *Trib*, which they still subscribe to because they like to keep up with Chicago news, arrives by mail, a few days late. They don't read the *local* papers, as Sara*h* calls them with disdain. They've been retired five years this spring, having stayed on at the university till they turned sixty-five. They were planning to travel some, at long last, that fall, when it was cooler. Then 9/11 happened. Now they are, they feel, too old.

A chilly April morning, and Sara*h* has lit the fire. She is reading Muriel Spark's obituary aloud to Sara B, immersed in Styles. Sara*h* enjoys obituaries. She lingers over the list of Spark's fiction. "We never read *The Comforters*, I don't believe."

"No," says Sara B. "You, *we*, decided it didn't have enough gravity. 'Better read the best books first . . . ' That was our motto, wasn't it. We didn't read *Miss Jean Brodie* either."

"Mmm," replies Sara*h*, "though we did see the movie. But maybe we should reconsider . . . ?"

"If you'd like," says Sara B, scanning the wedding announcements.

She pauses to look more closely at a picture of a cheerful young man and woman. She recognizes a name. An unusual name, Sara*h*'s married name, the one written on the atlas Sara*h* has kept all these years. The name belongs to the man, twenty-five or so if she has done the math correctly. This has to be Sara*h*'s grandson, she is suddenly sure of it. She wants to show Sara*h, Look, dear, look at this, you have family.* For Sara B has missed her own family all these years, not Stanley, not him; she misses the tiny daughters who played with matches while their daddy was out. Looks like they were playing dressup, the coroner said, making candle crowns, setting lighted wreaths of tulle and glitter on their heads. They must have seen it on TV is what the coroner said, people doing things like that. Years ago, she would slip away from work from time to time, leaving Sara*h* behind, and go to the cemetery where the little girls were buried. She never told Sara*h.* Sara*h,* she felt, would not have understood.

Now she aches to speak: *Look, right here! You have a grandson.* Maybe they might travel east, it's safer now to fly, isn't it, go see him, them? Feelings change, ugly feelings recede, do they not, after forty years? *It would be so nice . . .*

But then again, she has always been the sentimental one, like her mother.

Meanwhile, Sara*h* reads on. "And look: she lived with another woman. Penelope somebody. For years and years. Isn't that something."

"I didn't know . . . ," Sara B begins.

Sara*h* peers at her over half-moon glasses. "She was a lesbian? Is that what you were going to say? I don't think so. After all, look at us."

"Yes," Sara B replies, folding Styles neatly into a square and then a triangle, creating a little soldier's hat. Like the ones she made for the girls years ago, like the ones her mother made for her when she was small.

"Yes," she says again. "Look at us." She would like to weep, but instead she gets up, rather stiffly, and tips the paper hat into the fire.

Tyrone Power Is Dead

"On the Upper East Side," says Davida, for the second time. She's speaking to her mother on the pay phone in the dorm lobby, practically shouting. The connection is bad, staticky; her mother's voice crackles. "Yes, of course it's safe," says Davida, a far sight safer, she wants to add but doesn't, than the South Side neighborhood back home where she grew up.

Miranda has invited her to New York, Manhattan. Miranda is her roommate, a small, dark girl half her size who wears her hair in two braids tied with bows, like Margaret O'Brien, the former child star. Timid, insecure Miranda has made Davida her only friend. Davida is not sure of this friendship. Miranda is too intense, she feels, to be a comfort, which is what Davida has always assumed friends should be. Yes, to have fun with, but also to tell you everything is going to be okay when you think you're going to die from shame, or grief.

Davida is Miranda's friend, but Davida's not sure the reverse is true. Miranda, emotionally greedy, feasts on Davida's warmth and energy, her social ease, her charming facility for graceful conversation. These words do not come from Davida; Miranda has spoken them herself, telling Davida of her fascination. You remind me of Madame de Staël, Miranda told her. Said at dinner in the dorm, the day they first met. Miranda, brilliant and plain, has received a first-rate education; she's well-equipped to handle the rigors of the liberal arts college they both entered as freshmen some weeks ago. Beautiful and bright Davida, not even sure who Madame de Staël *is*, is even less sure she belongs at this college. Yet Miranda praises her, obviously adores being around her.

Yes, makes Davida feel good about herself. So good she's outscored Miranda on their first history test. This notable fact has attracted the attention of Miranda's mother, an imposing lawyer who visits her daughter weekly from a not-too-distant city to make sure her only child is progressing as expected. Miranda's mother supervised the decoration of the dorm room, displacing severe college furnishings with a Persian carpet, Tiffany lamps, matching escritoires and bombé commodes, and a pair of antique spindle beds topped with satin quilts. Miranda's mother thinks that Davida, wholesome Davida owing to her midwest birth and upbringing, is good for Miranda. And now she's offered a weekend in New York as a present to both girls. Opera, museums, the theatre—"The Lunts, my dears, are in town, you *must* see them"—they are all to be attended. Davida wonders if she'll have to submit a written report to Miranda's mother after the weekend is over.

She's told her mother they'll be staying with a friend of Miranda's mother. No, she doesn't know what Mrs. Friend's husband, yes, that's what her name really is, interesting, isn't it, she doesn't know what *Mr.* Friend does. I think they have lots of money, says Davida, truthfully. She does not tell her mother that Mrs. Friend is divorced. Her mother might get the wrong idea.

"Now pack carefully," her mother cautions. "Remember to bring your own washcloth."

The washcloth, unpacked and hung in Mrs. Friend's guest bath a few days later, becomes a source of amusement for Miranda.

They leave the college on Friday noon, after their last class of the week. Miranda's mother insists they take a cab to the train station and has sent Miranda money expressly for this purpose. She's given Miranda lots of money, for rail fare, for more cabs—"You girls must promise me that you will not, under any circumstances, ride on a bus"—and what she calls "refreshment," by which she means that the girls should take themselves to tea at the Plaza on Friday afternoon, after their arrival in the city. Mrs. Friend will be expecting them at her apartment at six-thirty. Miranda's mother has already arranged for a large arrangement of white roses, Mrs. Friend's favorite flower, to be delivered to Mrs. Friend's apartment shortly after their arrival. (This is years, *decades*, before Central America becomes Manhattan's cheap and prolific florist. When Davida, who is good at numbers and well aware of the cost of living, sees the bouquet, she calculates its cost and concludes that Miranda's mother has spent as much as two hundred Chicago dollars. Possibly more in New York currency. Nearly half a month's salary for Davida's father, a high school math teacher.)

The train ride is uneventful, except for a pesky old man wearing mismatched socks and a shiny brown suit. He appears from nowhere while Miranda is using the restroom and sits down next to Davida, who is reading *What Is to Be Done?* for political science. He puts a craggy, brown-speckled hand on her knee. Davida recoils. Undeterred, he moves his hand up her thigh. Davida whacks his hand with Lenin and he flees up the aisle, nimbler than she'd supposed. When Miranda returns they discuss Lenin for several minutes. (Miranda is not taking the same class but has studied the Russian Revolution in her progressive preparatory school.) Miranda then announces she's sleepy. She curls up, catlike, feet tucked beneath her, and lays her head on Davida's left arm. Davida, polite and left-handed, rides the rest of the way to New York unable to move.

"Never take the first cab," says Miranda. They emerge from Grand Central to contemplate a gray November drizzle. There are few cabs to be seen, and none without passengers. "My mother's rule," says oblivious Miranda. "And look for a Checker. They have those wonderful little swivel stools in back." Miranda is visibly excited. In her Best & Co. double-breasted blue coat with matching self-tied hat, red T-straps and white silk knee sox, Miranda could be a ten-year-old in from Scarsdale with her mother for an afternoon of shopping, followed by chocolate sundaes at Schrafft's. Davida doesn't know this then, of course, having never been to Manhattan before and knowing nothing of Schrafft's or the New York suburbs. But she does feel like Miranda's mother, though she looks more like the Seven Sisters college girl she is, in her black reefer coat and discreet, tasteful cloche and plain pumps with baby Louis heels; these are courtesy of Marshall Field's, part of her payment for being a member of Field's junior sales staff over the summer, a group of girls known as the College Board. She has a complete wardrobe from Field's, specially selected by Miss H, the board's grown-up adviser, for an eastern college. The girls going to Illinois and Michigan and the University of Denver got clothing with a somewhat different look, and, Davida suspects, a somewhat different price tag, too. Davida, eastward bound, was Miss H's pet.

Miranda is jumping up and down and grinning, clutching Davida's arm. "Oh, this is just *too* exciting, don't you agree?" she chirps. Having her mother at a greater distance seems to have done wonders for Miranda; Davida has never seen her so ebullient. Davida suppresses an ominous pang as they huddle at the station door, gazing at the rain and traffic and indifferent pedestrians pushing in all directions.

"We could probably walk," she suggests. The rain is light, they have umbrellas. She's memorized a map of the city, not all of it, only their destinations. The Plaza isn't that far, to Davida at least, used to trekking blocks and blocks through the Loop and South Shore and Hyde Park. Alone, she would have caught the uptown bus over on Fifth. But there's Miranda, and Miranda's mother. She looks down at Miranda, now subdued, holding ever more tightly to Davida's arm. "I don't think I can walk," Miranda whispers.

Davida decides to take charge. "We have to. Put up your umbrella." With Miranda reluctantly following, Davida picks up her suitcase, moves seamlessly into the streaming crowd, and heads west on Forty-second Street.

Mrs. Friend lives in the East Seventies, several doors off Fifth Avenue. She has her own home, not an apartment but a town house, Miranda has told Davida, preparing her for the visit. Four charming floors of gleaming wood, ornately carved antique furniture upholstered in jewel-hued silks, European porcelain, English silver, Impressionist pastels, a few Old Masters, collected over several generations. Davida, impressed, says it sounds like a museum. Oh, it is, says Miranda, who has visited several times with her mother. Davida wonders where Mrs. Friend's money comes from but does not ask. In the midwest you are taught not to ask about money, in the same way that you would not inquire about sex or religious practices. And in Mrs. Friend's case it's not at all a good idea to ask about sex, or religion either, at least not in the same sentence.

Mrs. Friend, Miranda has told Davida, is the former wife of a clergyman. Davida is not aware that clergymen make much money. Are they not supposed to live simple, tidy, selfless lives, accruing few possessions? Davida does not know this from experience, having not been taken to church much as a child by her vaguely Protestant parents; her knowledge of Christian ministers comes from Hardy, George Eliot, and Dostoevsky. You are naïve, Miranda tells her. Some ministers are very rich. They graduate from Harvard and Yale and have family money. They become ministers because they are not smart enough to be doctors or lawyers. Davida mentions primogeniture. That, too, says Miranda, except that their families usually have enough antiques and money to share with all the children.

Mrs. Friend's former husband, Miranda says, is an Episcopal minister. *Was*, she corrects herself. Although she supposes that technically he remains a minister, no matter what. The *what* in his case being substantial. She does not know the details, but Mrs. Friend obtained her divorce without difficulty in New York State, where adultery is the only legal ground, and her settlement included the town house and the furniture, porcelain, Old Masters, etc.

Miranda is telling Davida about Mrs. Friend at a coffee shop on West Forty-seventh Street, off Fifth. Davida has led them there because the rain has changed from drizzle to downpour. Miranda had suggested they look for a Schrafft's but was overruled by proximity. The coffee shop is not very clean. Miranda's mother wouldn't approve. A faint smear of someone else's lipstick rims Davida's coffee cup. Miranda is drinking hot chocolate from a chipped mug. They agree they will not mention this part of their visit to Miranda's mother. They also agree not to use the coffee shop bathroom. They will wait till they get to the Plaza.

They tack their way up Fifth, cautiously fording puddles when the rain subsides, retreating under store awnings when a new downpour breaches the mist. They slip into Tiffany's and spend much of an hour looking at china and silver flatware. A salesman, assuming Miranda to be Davida's little sister, and assuming Davida to be planning a wedding in the near future, asks Miranda if she will be the junior bridesmaid. Davida is still laughing when they reach Bonwit Teller. Davida tries on several dresses. Miranda, informed that Bonwit's has no children's department, sits on a sofa and watches Davida. They both use the bathroom.

When they reach East Seventy-eighth Street, it's after six-thirty. Davida believes she looks reasonably presentable, though her shoes feel slippery. Miranda, on the other hand, is a mess. Her grey-spattered knee sox sag, her coat is missing a button, and she has lost her hat. Probably, she thinks, in the coffee shop. A maid in black-and-white organdy answers the door, looks them over reprovingly and sends them upstairs, to bathe and change before Mrs. Friend sees them. She has guests, the maid informs them sternly, and they are preparing to leave for dinner.

The girls hurriedly pull themselves together in the guest suite on the second floor. They've been assigned separate rooms with a shared bath between. The rooms are furnished with canopied beds and marble-topped rosewood dressers adorned with nosegays in similar crystal vases. Descending twenty minutes later, careful not to disturb paintings and other artwork clustered along the staircase, Davida takes in the elegance, the opulent décor, and concludes that Mrs. Friend is very rich indeed.

Five adults are waiting in the foyer. Waiting for *them*. A short, plump woman in green silk and matching emerald earrings steps forward to embrace Miranda, murmuring words of welcome. And then Davida is introduced, first to plump and green Mrs. Friend, by Miranda, and then by Mrs. Friend to her other guests for the evening. A former senator, sixtyish, tall, silver-haired, wearing a camel polo coat; Davida knows his name from the newspapers. His companion is a novelist of modest repute, also grey-haired, in grey tweed over an ill-fitting navy dress, wearing glasses on a silver chain; plain and plain-speaking, though she seems cordial enough. Another couple are going out to dinner, too, younger, no more than forty, he in a velvet-lapeled overcoat, she in mink and Chanel. Davida sizes them up: rich and well-upholstered and ultimately nondescript; married to each other, though not happily. The maid assists Mrs. Friend with her own mink and out they go into the rainy night.

Mrs. Friend's chauffeur drives through the park at her direction, "so the girls can see it." Though not much can be seen on a rainy evening in November, only shifting patterns of light and darkness that flicker through rain-smeared windows. The girls are in the back seat, flanking Mrs. Friend. The other guests are following in a cab—a Checker cab, Miranda whispers to Davida, confirming her earlier wisdom. In her element now, Miranda seems more sure of herself, though her appearance hasn't improved much. Davida has loaned her a hat that's too big, it's crushing her ears and forcing her ribboned braids in odd directions. Five bright brass coat buttons call attention to their missing sibling. Curb splashes have stained a fresh pair of white silk knee socks, and Miranda's patent leather maryjanes are smudged. Davida, on the other hand, has received a silent but complimentary appraisal earlier from Mrs. Friend, in the foyer. Mrs. Friend appears to attribute their lateness to Miranda. Now Mrs. Friend and Davida chat easily about books, theatre, the Metropolitan Opera. Davida has had the foresight to read the previous Sunday *Times* and can therefore offer her own light commentary. She is careful to bring Miranda into the conversation. Tebaldi, Mrs. Friend remarks, will be singing Desdemona at tomorrow's matinee. "I hope you girls have tickets."

But they do not, says Miranda. Her mother has bought them Family Circle seats—the sound is much better there, Miranda says with confidence, echoing her mother—for the evening performance. "Oh, dear," says Mrs. Friend. *Butterfly* is on the bill for Saturday night, and it has, according to Mrs. Friend, a dreary cast. "But perhaps *Otello* was already sold out," Mrs. Friend offers, smoothing over. Miranda is mortified.

On the other hand, they are seeing *The Visit* tomorrow afternoon on Broadway. Mrs. Friend approves. "Dear Alfred and Lynne," says Mrs. Friend, "are not to be missed." The Lunts, it seems, are personal friends.

Their destination is a French restaurant on the West Side, in the Fifties. Intellectuals, artists, important people meet to dine there, Miranda whispers as they squeeze through the narrow entrance, past the bar crowded with chattering men and women hunched on high bentwood stools, into a synesthetic swirl of color, conversation, delicious smells of food and drink. Waiters in black and white weave briskly among tightly packed tables, scuffing up puffs of sawdust on the floor. She's seen nothing like this back home, no restaurant she's been to with parents, her own and her friends', has this vitality. Not Berghoff's or the Kungsholm or that dark Chinese place with garish paper lanterns on Clark Street whose name she can never remember, or Trader Vic's in Hyde Park, and definitely not the Cape Cod Room at the Drake, where she went with the other College Board girls for a farewell lunch. How, exactly, is it different, this restaurant? The people here *think* for a living, they have come to entertain each other with thoughts, ideas. They are not here to be distracted from life.

Mrs. Friend's maneuvering places Davida between the senator and the other male guest, who works on Wall Street. Across from her at the round table sits Miranda, wearing a navy wool jumper and Peter Pan blouse. Miranda will try, in vain, to catch her eye throughout the evening for affirmation, for reassurance. Miranda is flanked by Mrs. Friend and the broker's wife. The midlist author, who writes historical fiction, biographies of noted artists and musicians, is on the other side of the senator. The room is pleasantly noisy with vocalization, with collisions of flatware and crockery. Waiters squeezing past not infrequently bump. Conversation is difficult but the senator persists. With Davida. As does the broker, who tries to divide his attention between Davida and Mrs. Friend but is continuously distracted by his hostess. The senator ignores the author, who in turn ignores the wife of the broker. Who is forced to talk to Miranda through drinks—Miranda has a Shirley Temple, Davida a glass of Bordeaux at the senator's urging—and leek soup and grilled trout and dainty lemon tarts and tiny cups of strong coffee. Though not strong enough in Davida's case to overcome the effects of two or possibly three glasses of Pouilly-Fumé consumed with the trout.

The senator talks about books and paintings, Faulkner, Camus, Picasso. Davida, charming in pleated blue silk and pearls, mentions Lautrec. Oh, yes, says the senator, he too. The senator, as do all important men, likes an admiring audience. Davida obliges. The senator enjoys pointing out, not actually *pointing,* of course not, but indicating with a slight nod or a levitating eye, well known people, distinguished people, scattered around the room. No movie stars, nothing so vulgar, but there's the drama critic for the *Times* in that corner, near the bar, and the fat man a few tables over, why, that's Bunny Wilson, dining with his publisher. And the person being seated is William Inge. *Come Back, Little Sheba,* says Davida. Marvelous, says the senator. *Picnic,* too.

Several of the well known, not Wilson or Inge or the drama critic but equally celebrated in their own fields, stop by their own table, en route to the door or the restroom, to say hello to the senator or to Mrs. Friend or, once, to the author. Introductions are made, smiles and cheerful greetings exchanged, cheeks sometimes kissed, sometimes not. One of their visitors is an elderly, lumpy woman in black with flyaway grey hair framing a lined face, makeup-free. This is Madame T, wife of the prominent theologian, the senator informs Davida. Madame T's dress reveals crepey cleavage, at the base of which is pinned, rather incongruously, an enormous and quite droopy red rose. Davida, who has heard of the theologian, asks if he's in the restaurant with his wife. "I doubt it very much," says the senator dryly, and signals the waiter for more wine. In the ladies' room between courses, Miranda informs Davida that Madame T's husband has several mistresses. It's widely known, she says. A theologian? says Davida. Has mistresses?

Miranda is talking to her, Davida can hear her voice, something to do with breakfast. "Time to get up," says Miranda, patting her arm. "I let you sleep, but now you really must get up." Her voice is reproving, different from the usual ingratiating Miranda.

Davida forces her eyes open, wills herself, at Miranda's urging, to sit up, push back the silken bedclothes, bring her feet round and place them on the floor.

"You had a long night," says Miranda. "A very long night. But now it's nearly ten-thirty. Here—drink this." Miranda hands her a glassful of cloudy fizz, Alka-Seltzer maybe.

She drinks obediently, then rises slowly and heads for the bathroom.

"I'll bring you tea," says Miranda.

The play begins at two. They must leave for the theatre no later than one-fifteen. It's too late to do anything much before then, no time for shopping, barely time for a peek inside the Met Museum. They can have a quick lunch here, sandwiches, the cook has left a cold beef platter, fruit salad.

"We have tomorrow," Davida reminds her, buttering a piece of wheat toast. They are perched on stools in the kitchen, drawn up to a worn French farm table where the cook rolls out piecrust and chops vegetables. The cook has the day off. The maid is, presumably, in the maid's room downstairs. Mrs. Friend is out, attending a vestry meeting a few blocks away at St. James's.

"Tomorrow's the Whitney and MOMA," says Miranda. That tone again. A hint of petulance. More than that: disapproval. What has she done?

She hesitates before asking, "What time did I get in last night?"

"Two, " says Miranda. "We waited up. I did," she amends. "I was worried."

Davida decides to ignore this, for now. "And Mrs. Friend? Where was she?"

"In bed. She's not that young, you know," Miranda adds self-importantly. "She needs her rest."

"So *she* wasn't worried."

"Oh, she was *concerned*. Of course. But it was late, she'd had a long day. 'If anything happens,' that's what she said, 'if anything happens, you be sure to wake me.'"

"Presumably she didn't think anything *would* happen. . . . Who brought me home, by the way?"

"You don't remember," says Miranda, a statement confirming what she assumes is true.

"No, frankly, I don't." She refills her teacup. Tiffany Audubon. The kitchen china, according to Miranda. Davida and Miranda admired it in the store yesterday.

"A policeman. He said he found you outside, looking for the stairs." Hunched over on the stool, Miranda hugs her legs. Her knees are drawn up to her chin. She's wearing a child's plaid taffeta dress with a sash, matching bows on her braids, and a fresh pair of silk knee socks with her maryjanes, which the maid has cleaned. Davida is still in her bathrobe.

Davida sets the cup down carefully. "What are you talking about?"

"Oh, Davida!" Miranda slides off the stool and into Davida's lap. "Don't you know what happened? Can't you remember *anything*?" she wails.

Davida ponders this statement while Miranda settles herself, a procedure that concludes with Miranda dropping her head heavily on Davida's shoulder. Davida finds this annoying, but annoyance is superseded by rising panic. No, she realizes, she *can't* remember what happened last night. What happened after the senator claimed their coats at the restaurant, after they all, yes, all of them walked out onto West Fifth-sixth Street. Where was Miranda? Waiting with Mrs. Friend in front of the restaurant. Her car was coming soon, said Mrs. Friend. The author, the broker, the broker's wife, all three got into a cab. The senator said he'd drop her, Davida, off. Why? Why didn't she wait with Miranda and Mrs. Friend? "That's all right, dear, you go right ahead." Is she imagining this? Is that what Mrs. Friend said?

Miranda's mood has shifted. Now she's tearful. "You ignored me all evening," she sobs.

Davida feels guilty and embarrassed both.

"But you don't have to worry. I didn't tell Mrs. Friend. About the policeman, I mean. And I said you got in right after she went to bed." She looks up at Davida for reassurance. I was loyal to *you* is what she means. You abandoned *me*, but I didn't betray *you.*

Davida wonders if she's lost her mind. Or perhaps she's still in bed upstairs, asleep, dreaming. Or back at the dorm, and not in New York at all.

She eases Miranda off her lap. "I don't know what happened," she says, and goes upstairs to take a bath.

Earlier, using the toilet before coming down to breakfast, she's found streaks of blood on the tissue, blood smearing her pajamas. Her period. She hasn't brought Kotex, or a belt. She fumbles around in the bathroom cupboard and makes do with a napkin improvised from cotton batting and gauze. And then remembers her period isn't due for several weeks.

After breakfast she rinses her pajamas. In the bath she washes away smears of blood on her thighs, clotted blood on her pubic hair, the blood that's left. When she finishes there is no more blood.

They walk up Fifth to the Met. The rain has stopped but the day is grey and barren. They have half an hour, says Miranda. Only enough time to browse through Antiquities on the first floor, smooth statues of indolent Greek youths, clay pots with arcane histories, ornaments made from gold and precious stones, a model of the Parthenon in a glass case. Displayed next to the case is a photograph, grainy black and white, of schoolgirls from half a century ago, holding sketchpads and looking at this very model. How appealing they seem, Davida thinks, in their long coats and dainty buttoned shoes and floppy flowered hats resting lightly on heads of flowing hair. And wonders if somewhere, unseen, their picture is being taken, Davida and Miranda's, a picture of *them* visiting the museum. For posterity. But they look too odd together, do they not? And what would a picture of their visit commemorate, explain, to visitors fifty years hence? The schoolgirls stand for something, something she believes must be important, though she cannot say exactly what it is. Thought remains difficult, concentration impossible.

On the walk over, Miranda has tried to coax Davida's memory out of hiding. Did she have a good time? Was the senator interesting? Did they go to his apartment? Did Davida meet his wife? Yes, yes, yes, I don't think so, says Davida, smiling weakly, though truly she cannot remember.

"Well," says Miranda, "I guess you just had too much wine. More tea at lunch should make you feel better."

It does, sort of. It helps her stay awake through *The Visit*, an ageless story of love betrayed and betrayal avenged. The stars, husband-and-wife Alfred Lunt and Lynne Fontanne in what is rumored to be their final appearance on Broadway, transform a pedestrian plot into captivating drama. Miranda's words, murmured to Davida at intermission between sips of fresh orange juice served in a truncated cardboard cone. Davida has more tea, sweetened with too much sugar.

At the end Miranda insists on staying for every curtain call. Davida, on the aisle, excuses herself and uses the restroom. Miranda is flushed and breathless when she joins Davida at the door of the theatre. The best performance she's ever been to, Miranda says, keeping stride with Davida though not taking her arm now, the way she usually does when they walk together. The very very best.

Davida is not so sure. The Lunts were terrific, she agrees, but the play is troubling, don't you think? More than troubling: I was horrified, says Davida. To think that someone could actually have a person *killed* in such a heartless, premeditated way.

But she's had years to ponder what he did to her, after all, Miranda points out. He *ruined* her. Don't you think her revenge is justified? In the context of the play, of course.

But it's *wrong*, Davida insists. And he didn't *destroy* her, did he? She grows up, becomes a wealthy, celebrated actress.

Miranda shakes her head. Well, of course it's wrong, she says, and yes, the victim is now the conqueror, but Davida has missed the point of the play.

Everyone has a price, says Davida: obviously that's the point, or one of them. The rich old lady pays off the town's debts in exchange for the mayor's execution. But that's not her point. *Her* point is that it's a troubling play. And she's not convinced that everyone has a price. What a horrid thought!

It's great art and great theatre is Miranda's response. Davida, Miranda says for the third time in two days, is naïve.

On Broadway Davida, prompted by Miranda, hails a cab. A Checker cab. The girls climb into the backseat. Miranda sets herself down on the swivel stool and spins. Davida gives the driver their address. Not for the first time, Davida notices a disjunction in Miranda, physical and emotional Miranda both: a tiny figure in children's clothes but lacking innocence. She has the gnomish, fretful face of an old woman. It occurs to Davida that Miranda might have that rare disease, she can't remember its name, where children rapidly age into wizened elders. *Wizened*: a good word for Miranda.

The driver wants to chat.

"So you ladies been to the *thee-ah-tuh*?" he says, mocking their upper-class appearance. He has a crude voice, Davida thinks. The picture on his license, posted on the divider, shows a younger man, dark, unsmiling. Davida makes a mental note of the number and doesn't respond.

He catches Davida's eye in the rearview mirror. "You hear the news? Bet you don't know the latest."

No response.

"Ha, cat's got yer tongue I guess. Well, it's a biggy: Tyrone Power's dead. . . . Didja hear me? Tyrone Power the movie star. Dropped dead in Spain. On location. And just forty-four years old. Ain't that somethin'?"

"Don't say anything," Miranda whispers. "Mother says we shouldn't talk to cab drivers."

The cabby chatters on about Tyrone Power, up Broadway, across the park, all the way to East Seventy-eighth Street. Miranda doesn't give him a tip. He mutters something obscene and speeds away.

"You would have thought it was the President," says Miranda, climbing the stairs. "Or the Queen."

Davida, companion to her father at the movies since late infancy, mourns inwardly. *The Black Rose. Captain from Castille.* And just this summer, *Witness for the Prosecution.* A beautiful man. She'd take him over Alfred Lunt any day.

They have a light supper, creamed chicken on patty shells, with Mrs. Friend in the dining room, served by the maid. The dining room china service is Wedgwood. Mrs. Friend says she prepared the chicken herself. Mrs. Friend asks how they liked the play, and without waiting for their response delivers a monologue on the Lunts. Her friendship with Alfred and Lynne goes back twenty-some years. Many's the time she's had lunch, dinner, late-night drinks with them at the very place where they dined last night. Why, this very week they're coming over for tea; such a shame the girls won't be here to meet them.

And you, Davida dear, how did you enjoy your evening with the senator? Isn't he marvelous company? What an intellect! Did you know he's an authority on the Etruscans? But you must. I wanted you to see his fabulous art collection—that's why I had you go home with him last night. A lovely man. You don't find that sort of erudition in many politicians, I'm afraid. Though, of course, he's hardly a politician. He's more like Wilbur Cross, in politics out of a sense of duty—you girls do know who Wilbur Cross was, of course?

Miranda nods. Davida is mystified but tries to conceal it. Mystified by Wilbur Cross. By the senator's art collection, no. Memory, bits of it, is returning.

Wilbur was also a dear friend, though older, much older, of course, a friend of her parents. Wilbur was a literary scholar. Yale, Yale, Yale. But duty called. He was a fine governor. Of Connecticut, she adds, looking at Davida, whose ignorance must be showing.

"The senator can do a lot for you, dear," she says to Davida. "A great deal. You must keep in touch."

Miranda, presumably, needs no help.

Tyrone Power's death is not mentioned.

The opera is, as Mrs. Friend foretold, a disaster. Davida and Miranda arrive late, and have to wait in the lobby till the end of the first act. Finally seated in the Family Circle, they find it difficult to see the stage. The sound, on the other hand, as Miranda's mother foretold, is clear indeed. So clear that their ears hurt. Cio-Cio San shrieks, Suzuki bawls, Pinkerton wails, Sharpless bellows. The performance seems to Davida like a bad parody of Gilbert and Sullivan. They leave before the third act, Miranda saying she is tired, Davida relieved. They walk up Broadway, looking for a cab; any cab will do now. The evening papers have the story, big front-page headlines: TYRONE POWER DEAD. Davida would like to buy a *Mirror* but restrains herself. They are both in bed by ten-thirty.

There's an obit in the *Times* on Sunday morning, the headline glimpsed briefly by Davida before she hands the paper over to Miranda. The girls are reading in the front parlor. They've had orange juice, toast, and eggs, alone, in the kitchen. Mrs. Friend has gone to church. Miranda, who is Jewish, and Davida, by default, are exempt from attendance. Sunlight floods the parlor: the maid has drawn back heavy lined draperies and told the girls to make themselves comfortable. Eighteenth-century furniture does not offer much comfort, but Davida settles for a padded chair (Louis Quinze, according to Miranda) near the window. Davida reads the *Magazine* and the *Book Review*, allowing Miranda the first section. Half an hour later, Davida's finally able to see the obit. *Heart attack. Unexpected. Shock.* A list of the movies. The wives. A child.

Once upon a time that now seems very long ago, Davida dreamed of marrying Tyrone Power herself. But she would never tell this to Miranda.

On Sunday afternoon they do MOMA first, and then the Whitney, tours of duty, Davida feels, rather than pleasure. Because the weather's fair today, unusually fair for November, they stroll, at Miranda's suggestion, through Central Park. At sundown they're near the lake. Miranda, breaking a long silence, indicates silhouetted towers in the western sky, to the north. "The senator lives there," says Miranda. "As you know."

And Davida remembers everything.

The evening passes quickly: a kitchen supper alone—Mrs. Friend is at evensong—with little conversation, then schoolbooks, more Lenin for Davida, Jacob Burckhardt for Miranda. Followed by baths and bed. The maid awakens them early the next morning, and after a breakfast of toast and tea and cursory hugs from Mrs. Friend they are driven by her chauffeur to Grand Central. The girls have afternoon classes today, which they must attend.

There is distance between Davida and Miranda now, a growing formality. On the train they read their books. Only that evening, back at the dorm after dinner, does Miranda bring up the trip. Davida, she says, must write a thank you note to Mrs. Friend, and of course to Miranda's mother too. Miranda says this rather stiffly. Davida automatically says of course and settles herself at her escritoire for an evening of study. Miranda does not ask Davida if she enjoyed herself, and Davida does not volunteer appreciation of the weekend.

Desuetude. An awkward word, and Davida has never been sure how to use it. Until now. It comes to mind unsummoned, defining her new relationship with Miranda. *Sentence, please:* The friendship between Davida and Miranda has entered a period of desuetude.

The first call comes through at eight o'clock Monday evening. The hall phone rings three times before it's picked up, then a female voice shouts *"Davida!"* Who plunks down Lenin, dutifully emerges from her room, puts receiver to ear and hears a man's voice *purring,* yes that's the word, purring words, dirty words, words the cab driver used and worse. A pause. *Who is this?* But she doesn't have to ask. She knows. And hangs up the phone without speaking.

There have been boys, boys at home, nothing serious, though Davida promised to write a high school classmate who's gone west, to Stanford. But has not because she's heard nothing from him. In two months at college she's had five dates, *arrangements* the house mother calls them, with *approved* male escorts, Amherst, Williams, Penn boys. The one from Penn tried to put his tongue in her mouth, without success, at a party after a football game. He was drunk. Davida, sober and alert after two Cokes, deflected. Men are something of a mystery to Davida. Back home, she was too smart for most of the boys her age. Your time will come, her mother has always said. Don't rush things.

Miranda has had no dates in college. She has told Davida she went to three dances at her girls' preparatory school, with sons of her mother's friends. Miranda says you have to be careful about boys. Her mother's advice again. Oddly, Miranda's father is never mentioned. Absent? Dead? Miranda doesn't say. Davida doesn't ask. Perhaps he's in an institution, Davida's mother has suggested. Better not to ask. Missing fathers are like sex and religion.

The calls continue, four in all, till the college switchboard shuts down at ten p.m. The purring voice is cut off in midphrase, midword: *You cunning bi—*

After dinner on Tuesday, Davida goes to the library. When she returns to the dorm at eleven, she sees her name on the hall phone sheet six times, at intervals between seven and ten. *MNM*, dorm shorthand for *Male No Message,* is written on the first line, with ditto marks beneath and "same guy" penciled alongside.

Henceforth Davida spends every evening in the library. Miranda offers no comment on the situation. Nor does she invite Davida home for Thanksgiving. Davida spends the holiday with the housemother's family in the village. The purring calls persist for several weeks. Most are MNMs, though Davida picks up the phone a few times and hears the familiar voice. She tells no one. And then, suddenly, there are no more calls.

Davida begins to vomit in December, a week before vacation begins. Every morning she rises to waves of nausea and runs to the bathroom.

Miranda does not comment, nor does she offer comfort, or reassurance. Now she simply ignores Davida most of the time. Miranda, Davida has concluded, is not a friend. Nor is anyone else there, for that matter.

The college, Davida has learned, is not a friendly sort of place, at least to her. Oh, the girls are polite enough; good manners are enforced by the college code and the fussy housemother and the mannish dean and the president, who has a doctorate from Cambridge. Davida has chatted with the president at Sunday teas and thinks she's made a good impression. But no girl in her right mind would really *talk* to any of these women; secrets must be kept, as a sophomore hallmate put it one evening in the bathroom while they both were brushing their teeth. Those old birds take *in loco parentis* seriously, said the hallmate. Don't ever tell them a thing. The hallmate was being unusually generous with time and advice, but this was only a display of sophistication, Davida realized, not friendship. They expelled the girl who lived in your room last year, said the hallmate, after she talked to the dean. About what, Davida wanted to know. Sex, said the other girl, picking up her towel and toothbrush. She was out the door before Davida could ask more.

Most of the other girls have gone to private eastern secondary schools, share histories different from her own. Tell secrets to one another, Davida is sure of it. But not to her. They keep to themselves is how her mother would put it.

She decides not to go to the infirmary.

Back home on Christmas break, Davida conceals the nausea. Her period is now a month overdue. She says nothing to her mother, a former grade-school teacher from rural Iowa. Where her mother comes from, nice girls don't get pregnant. Or drunk either, for that matter. She wonders if her father knows, or suspects, but her father, thank heaven, is distracted. His prize trig student is suddenly taken ill, seriously ill, and her father frets about the boy. Her mother has worries of her own, mostly having to do with money, as Davida will learn eventually. And Davida, an only child, has never given either parent cause for concern. To them, beautiful, bright, self-assured Davida is perfect. Two weeks pass quickly, taken up with study and visiting friends. On New Year's day Davida is back on the train, returning to college for classes and semester exams.

She does not allow herself to think beyond that. And wills herself not to panic. Something, she tells herself, will arise to solve her problem.

And so it does. Her period, six weeks delayed, suddenly comes. That's how she prefers to think of it. The word *miscarriage* is distasteful and maybe, just maybe, inaccurate. She refuses to look at what emerges in the toilet on the third evening, after her English final. Six days later exams and the bleeding both end. She will not see a doctor. Generations of women have gone through this, have they not, without recourse to medical intervention? Olan comes to mind, Olan in *The Good Earth* bleeding in the rice fields. And refusing to stop work. Though perhaps Davida misremembers; maybe Olan delivered a full-term child. But it doesn't matter now.

Davida remains in the dorm over the brief semester break. Miranda goes to New York to stay with Mrs. Friend. Davida has never written thank-you notes to Mrs. Friend or Miranda's mother. This is not an oversight but the result of a conscious decision. The hallmate who warned her in the bathroom months ago is in Cuba during the break, having an abortion. Her roommate took up a collection. Davida was told and asked to contribute; sharing this secret is permissible, apparently, since money, lots of money, is needed. Davida has given five dollars, her self-allotted weekly spending money.

Davida will not be having a roommate next semester. Miranda's mother has ordered the college to find Miranda a single room. Davida returns from the library on the last day of break to find herself moved, too, to a gabled nook on the third floor. The college furniture is unattractive but serviceable.

A few times over the following months, say on a rainy Saturday afternoon when Davida's in her room studying, she finds herself staring out the window, looking at but not really seeing the smooth, tree-studded lawn beneath her, stretching half a mile down to the village. What *would* she have done, she wonders, had it turned out differently? Persuaded the girls to take up a collection for *her*? And if they didn't, then what?

Would revenge have been a possibility? Could she envision, years hence, doing what the old lady did in the play, devising a plan to ruin if not kill the senator? Once, a lifetime ago, she would not have thought so. Now she's not so sure.

The interruptions cease, eventually. Life goes on. She tells herself she will be all right.

Seduction is not difficult to explain, is it? Though Davida was not deliberately provocative, wore attractive but conservative clothing, did not engage in under-the-table knee grazing and was careful to keep her hands to herself, Davida could not help her beauty. Or glowing contentment, enhanced by Bordeaux and Pouilly-Fumé, by Jolie Madame swabbed at her wrists and ears, by melding aromas of grilled trout and lemon custard, *by the sheer delight she felt at being alive.* She remembers it all, even—no, *especially*—the crepe-bosomed Madame T and her drooping rose, will remember the evening the rest of her life, that part. That was *before.* What happened afterward, the senator's fumbling embraces, the brief drunken bedding, the senator passed out on the sofa, she dozing beside him for what? An hour? Hours? Then getting herself downstairs, ignoring the doorman's knowing leer when he put her into the taxi—all that will be nearly forgotten. To be remembered only on those rare occasions when she sees or hears the name of Tyrone Power.

As it happens, vengeance comes anyway, though not by her hand. In the fall of her senior year, the senator is killed in a plane crash. An especially gruesome plane crash that involves serpents and African swamps. Davida reads about it in the Sunday *Times.* Miranda, who rarely speaks to her now, mentions it at dinner. A dear, dear friend of my mother's, says Miranda to the table, blotting a tear. The other girls, who have long since learned to ignore Miranda, murmur a few false words of sympathy, then resume their chatter. Davida says nothing.

It's years later, their twenty-fifth reunion, and Miranda, still small and dark though apparently less socially insecure, is mingling at the president's reception. Everyone knows it's Miranda; even in dowdy grown-up clothes and ballet flats and grey-seamed hair hanging past her shoulders she looks the same. Miranda, say alumnae newsletters, has been ill, hospitalized for undisclosed ailments over the years. No mention of career, marriage, children. "I've been at McLean's," says Miranda, "on and off," to anyone who'll listen. Most of the other women are back at the college with husbands, or lovers. They nod at this intelligence and try to conceal embarrassment. "I had a nervous breakdown," Miranda adds, just in case she's been misunderstood. Miranda appears to be alone.

And now it's Davida's turn to be an audience. Miranda sidles over and stretches on tiptoes, attempting a light kiss on the cheek. Davida does not return the gesture. They have not spoken since college. Miranda has not attended previous reunions. Davida's husband, hearing Davida's *sotta voce* "Oh, dear!" at Miranda's approach, has left to refill punch cups after brief introductions.

"That was all my mother's doing," says Miranda abruptly, after mentioning McLean's and her breakdown. "I thought you should know."

Davida forces a tight smile. "I'm not sure what you're talking about."

"Oh, yes—you remember," says Miranda. "Our trip to New York. Freshman year. Mother was very old-fashioned, wasn't she? She's dead, by the way. Years ago."

Miranda fiddles with her hair. She's not wearing any jewelry, or makeup either. "Of course, Mrs. Friend, you remember her, the woman we stayed with, she and Mother told each other *everything*."

Davida looks around to find her husband. He's chatting with another husband or lover near the punch table.

"Mother said you didn't know how to behave, what were her words—'in polite society,' that's what she told me." Miranda laughs at this.

Davida's stomach is turning. "I don't think—" *this is the time to discuss this, do you?*

But Miranda hasn't stopped talking. "Mother went on about it for years. 'That roommate of yours,'" she says, mimicking her mother's haughty tone, "'that girl was not what we thought, was she?'"

Davida's husband is coming back, he's almost here, now he's handing Davida her punch.

Miranda looks up at him with a sly grin. "Your wife," she begins, "your wife and I were talking about old times." Her teeth are badly yellowed. Perhaps from medication, Davida thinks, resisting an urge to grab Miranda by the throat. "We were roommates once, briefly, freshman year," she continues.

"Miranda—"

"But then my mother decided Davida wasn't a good influence—"

"Miranda—!"

"And for such a silly reason, too: *Davida didn't write a thank-you note!*"

"Well, now, that's interesting," says Davida's husband, trying to look concerned.

"Very," says Davida, taking a deep breath. She slips an arm around her husband, forces a smile and says they must be going.

They're moving away when they hear Miranda's voice calling, "Let's be in touch, shall we?" but when Davida turns, Miranda is chatting up another couple.

"You roomed with that woman?" Davida's husband sounds doubtful.

"Believe it or not, I did," says Davida, trying to laugh but somehow not succeeding. "The dean's idea, I guess. But it didn't last. As you must have heard."

"I guess you were a naughty girl," he says. "Shame on you!" His tone is playful. He gives her an affectionate squeeze. "My, my. Didn't write a thank-you note. For shame, for shame . . . "

"Indeed," says Davida. "For shame."

Atonement

When the letter came, Alice was rearranging flowers at the pantry sink. Her birthday bouquet from the ladies at the club, delivered six days ago, drooping now toward death. She might be able to rescue a few of the astramarias, she thought, snipping off dried leaves from slimy stems, though she did not care much for their purplish shade, never had. Stems of statis, blue and white, might also be reclaimed. The deep pink roses, what variety were they? Memory eluded her more and more. They had been her favorites, once, and perhaps the ladies, led by Charlotte, of course, who led everything, had chosen them for just that reason. But they were shot, shedding random petals. Roses never lasted. What was that Frost line? *Nothing gold can stay.* Nor pink either, the real color of birth. Of life. Human life. She gathered them up, pricking her finger on a thorn, and dumped the lot into a stepcan under the sink. Fringes on the white carnations were beginning to brown and curl. But a few would do, in a smaller vase.

Then the letter came. The postman had to ring, because he had a package for Velma, who lived next door. Would she mind? Velma didn't appear to be at home. Or the maid was watching television again and hadn't heard the bell. She signed for the package and left it in the front hall. She would stop by Velma's later, when she walked Jiggs, and leave it on the back porch. She ought to look in on Velma anyway; Velma had no one anymore. She took the mail into the living room, moving toward a square of pale winter light that streamed through the casement windows. Bills, a few notices for charities she supported. One stiff cream envelope, hand-addressed in blue ink, in a script she thought she knew.

No one sent personal letters anymore, did they? The children and grandchildren phoned or e-mailed—two of the grands had bought her a small computer for Christmas and taught her how to use it, sort of. Notes, of course, she received those. Invitations to play bridge mostly; odd how the ladies still kept up that ritual of writing, when they might have phoned. And announcements of babies, great-grands now. She always sent a check.

She recognized Charlotte's address engraved in raised blue letters on the back flap. She moved over to the small rolltop, her desk, always, something to keep her writing things separate from Robert's, and picked up the ivory letter opener, its handle crested with a bit of silver. A map stamped with tiny letters spelling *Tasmania*. Robert had bought it for her . . . but when . . . ? Years ago, in Hobart. The Fifties, it must have been, not long after the war, before the children came. Robert liked adventure, romance, else why repeat the endless voyage through the Pacific? What must he have done there during the war? Survived, that was it, when so many had not. Now settling into the wingchair, and goodness, the crewel upholstery was really wearing thin, it needed replacing, she slipped the yellowed ivory blade through the flap and drew out the letter.

My dear . . . my dear . . . He was all bones, leaning forward, no muscle left to raise himself. Trying to tell her something, but the nurse patted him back against the pillows, smoothed the sheet over the sharp knees. It was warm in the room. Yes, of course it was warm: he had died in August and wanted the windows open. *My dear . . . my dear . . .* and then he had slipped away. Years now. He had tried to tell her something, and she had never known what, exactly. Though she suspected.

"Dear," Charlotte was saying to her. But it meant nothing special. Charlotte called everyone *dear.* "I do think you need better looking after. Your hair, for one thing." A week ago. They were stuffing envelopes down at the Red Cross building. "Mario could give you some tips." Charlotte, blond and fit at seventy-nine, played tennis, singles, twice a week. "Perhaps for your birthday . . . ?"

"No, no, but thanks anyway." Really, was her hair that bad? Honestly gray, she thought, and what was wrong with that? But Charlotte had been after her, and everyone else in the club, truth to tell, for years. Her hockey-stick personality, they called it; she'd played right wing at school, and there she was, sixty-odd years later, still charging down the field, so to speak, all eight willowy feet of her. No, surely she wasn't *that* tall; she only seemed to be.

"Well, dear, if we can't get you to try Mario's, then what about flowers? Something lavish, a huge bouquet." Charlotte's manicured hands, faintly brown-spotted, moved swiftly, sliding blood drive announcements into envelopes she had hand-addressed.

"Flowers would be nice," she murmured, and marveled at how fast, how clever, how relentlessly *young* Charlotte continued to be.

My dear, the letter began. Odd, no personal name there, she thought.

My dear, I must tell you something, and I must tell you in writing. It has haunted me for years, and of course we are not getting any younger, are we? I talked this over with Father Andrew, by the way, and he agrees with me that perhaps this is the right way.

Father Andrew was the new rector, unmarried. In his thirties. Father John had been so kind when she buried Robert, but Father John had retired two years ago. He lived in a nursing home for widowed clergy somewhere upstate. Had she sent him a Christmas card? She hoped so. Father Andrew seemed bored whenever she went to see him, shuffling papers, looking at his watch. He seemed uninterested in the problems of elderly women. Why was Charlotte bringing Father Andrew into this, whatever it was?

As you know, I am so very fond of you, and we have had such a strong friendship through the years.

Well, yes, she thought that was true. The club had brought them together.

And of course I was so very fond of dear Robert.

She knew that, of course. But Charlotte was fond of all men. And all women loved Robert. No surprise there. He was handsome and charming. At the end, no longer what he had once been, but still charming. It all seemed so very long ago. Robert had been dead for years . . . five? Six? And an invalid before that. It was all so long ago. She could barely remember.

Something tinkled. Jiggs, shaking himself awake from a nap in the kitchen, ambled stiffly into the room and lay at her feet. The metal tags on his red leather harness made a happy sound, she thought. Jiggs had been a present from Robert, before he had the stroke. She had always wanted a French bulldog, and Robert had given her one for her birthday. There had been goldens before, long before, when the children were there. Robert loved retrievers. She preferred small dogs, dogs to be sat upon laps and cradled. She reached down and stroked his warm coat. Greying about the muzzle, and the vet had said he was going blind. Twelve . . . she was sure of that number. Old for the breed. Old for any dog.

She picked up the letter again, readjusted her glasses, and read it afresh, from the start. Goodness, what was Charlotte getting at?

. . . I don't believe you ever knew, but Robert and I were in love.

A small knot of pain formed somewhere near her heart, began spreading through her stomach, lungs, throat. It was old pain, remembered pain.

I know now that it was wrong, that we should not have hurt you so, dear. Father Andrew helped me see this. I went to him and asked what I could do to help you. I told him you were still grieving—imagine, after so many years! Goodness knows, I buried my Walter without regrets. He had a full life, I told myself. There was nothing left inside me that he could hurt. Did you . . . ? But of course not—silly of me to wonder! We always called you the Mouse, remember? So shy. We used to say "Alice the Mouse never knew any man but Robert, that's for certain!"

She put down the letter. Why was Charlotte doing this? She herself had not been blind. She and everybody else had known about Walter's flings, that's what they called them back then. And Robert's, too. The Mouse. Sweet, kind, obedient . . . Men were more discreet, once upon a time, but now it was out, it was all over the place these days, people tumbled into bed all the time with one another, men, women, married, single, it didn't seem to matter anymore and no one really gave a hoot. But she had. Well, not hooted. But been hurt, deeply hurt, the first time she found out. Robert's secretary. But of course she had been so busy with the children then . . . Margaret teething; Jim, who stuttered, needing extra attention because Robert was hardly ever home. And then she'd had the miscarriage, which brought them back together somehow, at least for a time . . . Of course she had known about Charlotte. Every husband in town had been to bed with Charlotte.

She never knew any man but Robert . . . Oh, but she had, she had. The memory was strong, of gin and Canoe and Joy commingled, of Walter kissing her cheeks, neck, caressing her breasts with warm hands, Walter raising her dress, pressing into her . . . covering her mouth with his lips, hushing her joyous cries.

It had never happened again. But no matter. Walter had saved her. Walter, in the country club cloakroom on a winter night, was it the Christmas dance? It must have been. Or maybe Valentine's Day. Walter had made her feel beautiful, desirable. Something Robert could no longer do. Because after the secretary, after the miscarriage, after Charlotte and the others, Robert had had a terrible accident. Lucky to have survived at all, that's what the doctors said, looking at pictures of the crumpled Rambler. A fluke, the way the stick shift had pierced his lower torso. No more children. But they were so lucky, weren't they, because they had two, one of each.

Jiggs stirred, and his tags tinkled like a summons for tea. Well, it *was* almost teatime. The winter sunlight had faded. Nearly four o'clock and time for his walk.

But first she must finish the letter. Again she wondered: Why had Charlotte written? To make a confession? To hurt her? Perhaps both? The Mouse. Sweet, shy, obedient. And naïve. Or so they all thought. All the old dears in the club. But hardly any left, besides Charlotte and herself. Mary Frances, Dorothy, Eleanor. And Velma and Katherine and a half dozen more. That made thirteen. None of the younger people wanted to join. The next generation, Margaret and Jim's, had other things to do with their time. The grandchildren weren't joiners. Who will do the good work when we go? they wondered aloud to one another at the Red Cross and the hospital, which seemed these days the only places where old women—there, she'd said it: *old women—w*ere needed and welcomed.

So, my dear, I just wanted you to know. I want, at the end, for there to be peace between us.

That was all.

With Jiggs at her heels she went to the hall for her coat and the leash. Somehow she didn't feel like seeing Velma now, deaf and forgetful. The package could wait.

She buttoned Jiggs into his red sweater and stepped out the door into the fading light. Charlotte's house was just up the hill. She would stop and knock on the door, make sure everything was all right. She headed up the winding lane, past slate-roofed Tudors and columned, shuttered colonials set back on spacious lawns and framed with massive skeletal oaks. A beautiful neighborhood in a lovely little town. A suburb, technically, but really a cozy, self-contained community. She had been happy here.

As Jiggs paused every few feet to sniff and scratch, she considered what she would say. Would this be only a look-in, a checkup disguised as a social call? Or should she say something about the letter? But what, exactly? *You've never known this, but your husband and I made love, just once, long ago.* Somehow she didn't think she could manage that, and besides, what was the point? And then it occurred to her: Perhaps Charlotte had sent similar letters to all the other women, all the old dears, all the ones who were left.

She reached the top of the hill and saw cars parked in Charlotte's driveway. And in front of Charlotte's house. She recognized some of them: Dorothy's red Buick, Katherine's aging beige Volvo. A Lexus, Eleanor's.

Father Andrew answered the door. Dorothy and Mary Frances hovered behind him.

"Perhaps you could leave the dog outside." It was an order, not a suggestion.

"But what is it? What's happened?" Her hand tightened on the leash.

"We think she took her own life," he said.

"But why?" She felt cold tears on her face.

"She left a note," said Dorothy. "Yes. A note," said Mary Frances.

"She had cancer," said Father Andrew, still not inviting her inside.

"'*I have cancer and I don't want to live anymore.*' That's what she wrote," said Mary Frances.

No one else was crying.

"Oh, my," she said. She took a step forward, but Father Andrew held the door.

"I think you'd better take the dog home first. There'll be an ambulance here soon. Now, if you don't mind . . ."

"Where are the others?"

"Back inside," said Dorothy. "Eleanor found her."

"I found her, too," said Mary Frances.

"We all did," said Dorothy.

"That's not true!"

She turned away and headed down the walk.

"Bridge tomorrow, ten sharp!" Mary Frances called after her. "Don't forget!"

She walked for an hour with Jiggs, up and down the hilly neighborhood, as twilight faded into darkness. Numb with cold she turned at last toward home. An ambulance sat with the motor running in Charlotte's driveway.

At suppertime she discovered the flowers, strewn in the pantry sink, limp and beyond revival.

Something to Tell You

You would not remember me. What I looked like, I mean. But of course not. You were two years old, last time I saw you, squirming in your father's lap. And that was fifty years ago. You wore a pink snowsuit, not the kind they have today, made of that puffy shiny polysomething. Wool, real wool. Pink. Snug leggings secured with elastic straps that looped under your Stride Rite baby shoes, a little jacket buttoned to your chin. Your blond hair—both your parents were blonds, Swedes way back, with blue eyes the color of cornflowers that grew wild back then by the road where we lived—your blond hair compressed in a matching pink wool cap that tied under your chin with a velvet ribbon. You were a fetching little thing. Your mother loved you. Your mother dressed you well.

My father had died. I was home from college half a continent away. You sat in your father's lap in the living room. Your father was offering condolences to my mother. *Your* mother did not come. Could not, said your father. *Under the weather* was what he said. Your big brothers—four of them, imagine that!—were, I suppose, at school. *The change*, said my mother later. That's what he meant: she was going through the change.

You were a late baby, perhaps unplanned. But your mother adored you. Please know that: Your mother adored you.

I read about it in the newspaper. It made all the papers, all the Chicago papers at the time: *Trib, Sun-Times, Daily News, Herald-American.* Suburban papers too, I guess, ones that covered our town. I saw it in the *Trib*. I didn't live in Chicago then or anywhere near. Chicagoland, that's what they called it, Cook County and a few places that clung around the perimeter. But I read the *Trib* every day in the library. Of course it was already three days old. But I made a point of reading it. I guess for reasons of nostalgia. I was in grad school at the time. You were nine years old.

They must have kept it from you, best I can figure. They must have made up some fantastic story. Or maybe you were away. That's right, I remember: you were on a sleepover, at a friend's house. The paper said so. I'm glad you had friends. I hope you had a normal life, something close to normal anyway. Before it happened.

Your mother died. That's what they must have told you. Your mother died and has gone to heaven. You were Lutherans, as I recall. That would have made sense, the part about going to heaven I mean. I guess that's comforting to a child, heaven, Jesus with the lambs.

But you must have noticed the scars on Tim's throat, after he came home from the hospital. What did they tell you? That he had to have an operation on his neck? But you were nine. I guess you believed them, or wanted to. And you missed your mother. I guess you didn't see the connection.

I loved your mother the way your mother loved you. I think you must have loved your mother back. Your mother was everything my own mother was not. Kind, warm, with a generous spirit. I think she loved me, though not in the same way that she loved you, of course not. Once, she gave me a charm bracelet with a little glass ball attached that held a mustard seed, and another time a small purse in navy blue kid with a lacy handkerchief tucked inside. There were other presents too, at birthdays and Christmas. I took care of your hamsters, the family hamsters, when you went away every summer. Not *you* or *your* hamsters, of course: this was before there *was* you. I babysat for your brothers, in grade school and high school. They were a rowdy lot, your brothers. The eldest, Bob and Jerry, locked me in the cellar once, and another time they glued my homework pages together. The younger two, Ralph and Tim, came along a year apart when I was in high school. I changed their diapers and read them *Pat the Bunny* and kept Jerry away. Jerry liked to pinch Ralph and Tim. He was jealous, I think. Tim, everyone said, was a handful. That's what people said back then when what they meant was *that boy is sheer trouble.*

You arrived in the spring of my senior year. I sat for you, as well as the boys of course, a few times, but I got a real job in June, after graduation. I didn't have time to babysit any more. She was so happy to have a girl, your mother was. She adored you. Please know that.

You won't find the stories today. Not unless you go to a big-city library and spend the hours it takes to spool through reels of microfilm. Assuming the library has Chicago papers on microfilm from that long ago. The stories aren't online. I know: I Googled your mother's name and the date and the town and all the words I could think of that might be pertinent—suicide, tragedy, attempted murder. "Sprawling ranch" too. Because I remember that's what the *Trib* reported. It was in the headline: MOTHER SLASHES SON, KILLS SELF IN SPRAWLING SUBURBAN RANCH. They called it a *sprawling suburban ranch house* in the article itself. I don't recall that your house was that large. Four bedrooms, but two were small. One and a half baths. A tiny den where your father read the paper every evening and smoked his pipe while your mother fixed pork chops or baked a chicken for dinner. Not sprawling by today's standards. Journalistic hyperbole.

I should finish my sentences and my thoughts. I Googled but found nothing. The story had disappeared. As though it had never happened.

I have never looked at the microfilm. Perhaps the story is not there either.

But you have to believe me. It really happened.

Is there "a need to know"? Is it your right to learn what happened? Well, yes, I would argue. Yes. But not because I share the views of those ranters on TV, people who demand answers to everything, deny a person's right to privacy. This is not a privacy issue. In any case no one else has to know. No one outside your family. *It's for your own good.* I mean that. And Tim's.

No one has ever told you. Either of you. Because if Tim remembered he would have said something to you, right? He would have been eleven, as I recall, when it happened. So he must have blocked it out. I guess his scars, the ones on his skin, faded. But somewhere there's a particle of memory lodged in his brain that nudges consciousness from time to time. And when that happens he pours himself still another drink. Loses his temper at still another boss and loses still another job. Moves to still another town to start over. Tries shrink after shrink, then never goes back because goddammit that person, he, she, will never understand. Except that Tim can't quite figure out what it is he wants understood.

Bob was killed in Vietnam. Jerry, never sociable, moved to Australia after college, still lives on a sheep station. I know this from your Christmas cards. I got back in touch with you twenty years ago. I had to know what happened to all of you. The rest of you. After I read about Ralph in the paper. Ralph made the national news, even the *Times.* Had a scrap of video on CNN. And then something else happened, something big, the *Exxon Valdez* spill I think it was, and Ralph wasn't news anymore. I know you were relieved. I guess you still visit him in prison; you don't say anything about him anymore in your Christmas card.

You have done well. You have never married. Never had children. By deliberate choice is what I think you told me. But I repeat: you have done well. You have a job, a career in fact. Friends. You cook, you ski, you own a dog. You give blood to the Red Cross and cash to Oxfam, leave minimal carbon footprints, do not own a handgun. An admirable citizen. You have turned out best of all.

And yet you look so sad in that picture you send each year. No smiles. Thin, almost frail. A resemblance to your mother, but she smiled. Always. Though at the end I imagine there were no smiles left to give.

You are now fifty-something, two by my calculations. You have outlived your mother by four years. There must have been rumors, growing up. Though your father remarried, moved to another town, you told me so. The story quickly became old news, I guess, like drug-crazed Ralph holding up that jewelry store. I don't think he meant to shoot, I really don't. It was the pot and coke and smack and whatever else he was trying on for size. I know the lawyer argued for clemency because of the drugs. Because of PTSD or whatever they called it then. Flashbacks. He'd enlisted at the tail end of the war. Avenging Bob's death I think is what you told me. Or maybe I read that in the paper too.

You do not have to tell Ralph when you see him. I'm a bit surprised that the papers didn't dig up the story about your mother and Tim when the Ralph thing happened. You know: a family history of violence, that sort of thing. But as I said, it's not on Google, so how would they have found out twenty years ago, before Google?

I hope you will not hate me, but I feel you must know what happened. And so here, at last, I will tell you the story.

Violation

"The odor is putrid, wouldn't you agree." Ronald, leaning over the sink, sharpened pencils.

"Mmmm," said Mina noncommittally, folding laundry at the kitchen table.

She had noticed it hours ago, making her early morning tea. Now it was stronger. A garbage smell, fetid. Fecal? Feral? Had some small animal, trapped inaccessibly in the floorboards, begun to decompose? Intense in the kitchen, the odor made its diminishing way into the dining room and through the front parlor and up the stairs to their bedroom and the nursery and the room behind the baby's room that Ronald used for his office.

Please don't let the shavings go down the drain, Mina wanted to say. Instead she bit down hard on her lower lip, a habit now when Ronald annoyed her. The lip was speckled with faint scabs.

The baby, Mildred, cried. She was lying in a bassinet in the dining room, a small space without furniture hunched against the kitchen. It was no more than a passageway to the front parlor. There was no back parlor, but the man from the university real estate office who rented them their half of the house had called the living room the front parlor and so they called it by that name too. It had a wood stove that Mina and Ronald were afraid to use. Or rather Mina was afraid. The house was cold; the radiators, crusted with peeling brown paint, gave off a frightful sound of hammering when the thermostat switched on but never got hot enough to warm the rooms. The stove might have helped, but then Mina would have had to find wood, and besides, she worried about carbon monoxide. Ronald, immersed in his books and wearing thick wool Bean sweaters sent by his mother, paid no attention.

Mina spent most of her time in the kitchen. She cooked and cleaned and did the laundry—an old Kenmore washer and dryer that came with the house sat in an alcove next to the sink—and ironed shirts for Ronald to wear to his seminars. Between these chores she sat at the bare wood table proofreading book galleys, rhythmically scanning lines of type with a Col-erase Blue pencil.

The baby gave out another cry. Mina always called her "Baby" when Ronald wasn't around. Mina had fed and changed Baby and put her down for a nap. Perhaps Baby was cold, though Mina had pushed her bassinet as close as she dared to the flaking radiator. Mina had dressed Baby in an extra sweater, and put newspapers between the blankets, for insulation. Maybe that wasn't enough. Maybe when Ronald went back upstairs she would turn on the oven and move Baby into the kitchen.

But Ronald was not going upstairs. He had brought down his briefcase and dropped it on the floor. "That odor," Ronald again protested, inspecting a pencil. "Can't you do anything about it? I bet it's *she*."

Mina, folding one of Ronald's undershirts, paused to chew at a hangnail. "Maybe," said Mina. "But *she*'s at work. The children are in school. I'll try her this evening."

Ronald's seminar was at three. It was now one-thirty. "I can't stand this," said Ronald. "I'm going to the library." He dropped the pencils into his briefcase and buckled the flap. The case, made of smoothly tanned golden calfskin, had been a present from his mother. Without flicking a glance at whimpering Baby, Ronald walked into the front parlor and took his jacket and astrakhan hat from the coat tree at the door. The Barbour jacket, dull green with a black velvet collar, was new, another gift from Ronald's mother. The hat, made of cropped black fur, made Ronald look vaguely like the Shah of Iran; he had worn it when Mina first met him, half a dozen years ago in New York. Then it had seemed chic; a less-clichéd alternative to berets worn by other graduate students. Here in the Midwest she thought it looked silly. But said nothing.

She was Dorothy, the other duplex tenant. A caramel-colored woman with straightened mahogany hair molded into a stiff bun, Dorothy worked as a typist in the math department at the university. She had three school-age children. Probably by different fathers, Ronald sniffed when he first saw them. That had been on the Saturday when they moved in, five weeks ago. Ronelle's skin was dark, much darker than her hair, as dark as the paint on the radiators. Ronald, annoyed by the similarity of the girl's name to his own, was annoyed even more by Ronelle's pointing out the similarity when they introduced themselves. Ronelle had two younger brothers, fraternal twins, eight-year-olds named Danny and Darwin; they were light-skinned like their mother but with inky black hair, close-cropped, like Ronald's astrakhan hat. Our mulatto neighbors, Ronald called them.

Mina and Ronald saw little of Dorothy and her children. "They keep to themselves" is how Ronald put it, when his mother asked him who shared the house. Ronald had phoned to give his mother their new address. Ronald did not tell his mother, who lived in New York, that they had Negroes living next door. Ronald's mother was southern; the *near* South, as Ronald put it, which meant Virginia and a higher class of people, according to Ronald, *educated* people. Which to Mina, who had no southern roots, meant viewing colored people like anyone else. She had been mistaken. Ronald's mother had left Virginia and come north after marriage, before Ronald was born; what a shock it was, she confided to Mina early on, after a third old-fashioned—Mina had invited her to lunch at Schrafft's, soon after becoming engaged to Ronald—such a shock to see colored and white *intermingling*, on the streets, in shops, riding the bus, right *here*, in this very restaurant. Though of course she had gotten used to it, everyone had to get used to it. Her voice, thickened by years of Camels, carried. Mina winced, though probably no one else was paying attention.

This was Ronald's third graduate program. He was forty years old. He had two partial master's degrees, one in English literature and another in psychology, from NYU. He had passed written exams but not completed a thesis for the first; he had only attended classes for the second. Philosophy had been Ronald's undergraduate major, at a second-tier eastern college; he had been accepted conditionally at this third-tier midwestern university for a doctoral program, the condition being that he complete one of the master's degrees. Ronald could not decide which he wanted to finish. Would it be Yeats? Or Jung? He had years to do this, Ronald told Mina. Years of proofreading, thought Mina, who had once been a graduate student herself. Diplomatic history at Columbia. She did not, she thought, want a degree from this midwestern university. Not that she had any time for study: housework and Baby and the galleys she picked up weekly from the college press were all she could manage for now. And if she had extra hours to spare, she needed to fill them with additional work, paying work. Her savings, from her former job at a publishing house in Manhattan, were covering most of the bills. Ronald's mother sent clothes for Ronald, jackets and ties and shoes from Brooks and Saks; and sometimes a check, usually for ten dollars, which Ronald used to buy pencils and typing paper and tobacco. He had recently taken up pipe smoking.

Ronald had seminars four afternoons a week. He slept till noon most days, then showered and dressed and ate a grilled-cheese sandwich that Mina took up to his study, tiptoeing in as he pored over the afternoon reading. He underlined passages, lots of them, Mina noticed, in pencil and drew little stars in the margins. Sometimes, when Ronald had many pages of reading to complete, he spent the night on the couch in his study, bought, like the other furniture in the house, from the previous tenant.

His name was David, and he had a wife and two small children. David had also been a graduate student in the philosophy department. David had been asked to leave suddenly, for reasons not publicly disclosed, enabling Ronald and Mina to move out of their single room with a shared bath in married student housing halfway into the semester. Houses close to the university with cheap rents were hard to come by; Mina was grateful for David's departure and had thus not spent much time concerning herself with David, or with David's wife and children. But a few weeks ago, at the department Christmas party, she had heard a group of women, student wives, whispering about David. *Lewd acts, exposing himself* is what she thought they said. But the wives hushed up when she drew closer, eavesdropping. She did not mention this to Ronald. Though the news disturbed her. Though perhaps Ronald already knew.

Baby had been Mina's idea; Ronald had reluctantly said okay, as long as Mina understood that a child was *her* responsibility. Though he had insisted that the baby be named Mildred, after his mother. Mina demurred—"It's 1965; no one names girls Mildred anymore"—but Ronald was adamant. His mother would be flattered, he said; his mother would write checks to support her namesake. This had turned out not to be the case; Ronald's mother paid no attention to Baby Mildred, and additional checks were not forthcoming. Mina thought she knew the reason: Ronald's mother believed that Mina wasn't good enough for Ronald.

Mina had no family to speak of, and no money, other than what she earned and saved, and no prospect of coming into money. Though she had gone to Bryn Mawr, she had been a scholarship girl; neither fact impressed Ronald's mother, who had spent a few weeks at a southern finishing school before eloping with Ronald's father. The marriage had fizzled, as had most of Ronald's family's money, both sides' worth. Mildred Senior lived in the Village and pretended to paint. She lived on a small allowance from trust funds left by a great-uncle who had worked at the State Department. Under Franklin Roosevelt and very high up, Ronald had told Mina, though vague about details. Mina the diplomatic historian had never heard of the great-uncle.

The smell, Mina noticed, was strongest by the basement door, at the far end of the kitchen. Willing herself to ignore it, Mina removed Ronald's pencil shavings from the sink. Baby was crying, nonstop. Maybe, Mina mused, Baby does not like this house either. But Baby, in all her eight months of life, had never been happy. Brought home from the hospital to their Brooklyn flat, Baby screamed continually (not continu*ously*; there *were* breaks, noted mindful Mina, ever the pedant). Perhaps it's colic, said the pediatrician, looking suspiciously at Mina, who wasn't breastfeeding. She had found it disgusting when the nurse made her try it in the hospital, the slurping and slobbering, the sticky little gums gnawing at her nipples. Switching formulas had helped, a little; the screaming stopped, but Baby was far from placid. She whimpered and whined, twitched in her fitful sleep, rarely smiled. Mina wondered if

Ronald had been this sort of infant. Ronald was fretful and twitchy, certainly, though of course he never cried.

Mina twisted the last pair of Ronald's argyle socks into a tight ball and then turned her attention to red-faced, howling Baby, who had worked herself into a fury of sweat and spittle. It is truly a wonder, Mina thought, that infanticide is not more common. "Let's take a walk," she said, lifting Baby out of her bassinet. Baby stiffened in Mina's arms and scowled. Mina slung her to the side, so that she rode Mina's right hip. "Let's see what we can find, shall we?" Baby snuffled and snorted and took several gulping breaths, replenishing air.

Mina had avoided the basement. She had never been down the stairs concealed behind the door. Nor, to her knowledge, had Ronald. Presumably it held the furnace and lots of pipes to carry steam upstairs.

She opened the door, found a light switch on the stairwell, headed down.

The basement was a smallish room, dim and dusty, dun-colored in the half-light. Thick rusting pipes draped with cobwebs crisscrossed the low ceiling. What she assumed was the furnace stood off to the side, a tentacled hydra swathed in gray asbestos. At the back were a pair of old laundry tubs and a fat wringer-washer, the kind she remembered seeing at her grandmother's farm. *She had been there a few times, taken by the aunt who raised her for a time after her parents died. Her grandmother spread newspapers everywhere, on the linoleum kitchen floor, on the carpets in the parlor, keeping everything clean she said. Mina squatted on the floor to read the headlines. "Where's Japan?" she had asked her aunt later, on the way home.*

Mina moved about the room, sniffing the air. Baby hiccupped and writhed. The smell was strongest in the farthest corner, by a door. Leading where, wondered Mina, turning the handle. A dim light glowed in the crack, revealing the basement on the other side of the house. Another asbestos-clad furnace, a pair of washtubs, a wringer-washer with a half-wrung sheet trapped in its arm. On the far wall a door stood slightly ajar, revealing steps leading upstairs. The smell must be coming from Dorothy's kitchen. But Baby was fussing. Mina went no further.

“Pee-*yoo*,” said Ronald, removing his coat and hat and hanging them neatly on the bentwood rack. “Did you call?”

“I tried. No one’s home.”

Ronald followed Mina out to the kitchen. Baby slept on by the radiator, tired out from her afternoon outing. Mina had pushed Baby in her carriage to Hamson’s Market on the other side of town, a precious place with polished wood floors, cured sausages hanging from the ceiling, bins of expensive wine nestled in sawdust. It was patronized mostly by the wives of full professors. Foodtown did not sell gruyère or Pepperidge Farm Whole Wheat, both of which Ronald required for his grilled cheese sandwiches. Mina had bought cheese and bread and two lamb chops for Ronald’s dinner. The lamb chops cost three hours’ worth of proofreading. Mina walked whenever she could, to save gas money.

“It’s Friday,” said Ronald, washing his hands at the sink. “Which means she won’t be back till Sunday night.” Dorothy took the children to Indianapolis on weekends; Ronelle had volunteered this information with a shy grin the day they moved in.

Mina turned lamb chops in the skillet. Pellets of grease stung her hand. “It’s probably coming from her kitchen,” she said, and told Ronald how she had gone downstairs and found the door that led to Dorothy’s half of the house.

“I’ll check it out after dinner,” said Ronald.

At first Mina had liked Ronald for his fussiness. Though she didn’t see it as fussiness then. He was neat, tidy, precise. Clean; immaculately so. Interested in her dissertation. Though later she learned that Ronald was interested in everything. That he was thirty-four years old and had no job did not offend her, not at first. Indeed, it was impressive: Ronald was not bourgeois; Ronald pursued truth.

“Chicken,” said Ronald. “Spoiled chicken.”

He closed the basement door behind him.

“She left packages of Foodtown chicken on the sink. I put them in the trash.” He wrinkled his nose when he said *Foodtown*. Back in New York, he had shopped at Gristede’s and had the Pepperidge Farm and the lamb chops and whatnot delivered.

“Won’t she know?” said Mina.

"She must have left a few days ago," said Ronald.

"But won't she know?" Mina persisted. "That you entered her house?"

"Who cares?" said Ronald. "It's disgusting. *She*'s disgusting."

Saturday was uneventful, which is to say that life continued. Baby alternately screamed and fretted, Ronald read and twitched and ate. Mina accommodated, changing diapers, cooking Ronald's meals, proofreading galleys. *Orchids: The Incredible Journey*, by a botany professor at the university. Mina had gone to the library, wheeling Baby in her carriage, to check on spellings. And discovered that Professor Llabbattarrya had copied most of his manuscript from a text published in 1937: *Orchids: Their Provenance*. The least she could do was make sure that the spellings were correct. Matched.

At dinner—supper is what it was, but Ronald said, most emphatically, that the evening meal was *dinner*—Ronald was grumpy.

"*Spaghetti?"* said Ronald. "And why am I being served spaghetti?"

"Our money is running out," said Mina.

"Meaning?" said Ronald.

"That we—you—can't afford to dine on lamb chops and filet every night."

Ronald *harrumphed*, like an elephant trumpeting. They—no, she—had taken Baby to the zoo soon after their arrival. To see the babies, elephants, giraffes, a tiny rhino pasted with mud. Sixty miles to the nearest city, round trip. A tank of precious gas. Ronald spent the afternoon taking a nap.

Mina had made a Linzertorte for dessert. "This raspberry jam isn't up to snuff," said Ronald, probing with his fork. "How many times have I told you: You can't shop at Foodtown. If they don't have what we need at Hamson's, then you'll just have to go to Indianapolis."

"Or maybe Chicago?" said Mina, scraping most of Ronald's spaghetti into the trash bin.

Ronald ignored her. Wiping his mouth daintily, he stood up. "I'm going to have another look," he said, and headed for the basement door.

"What for?" said Mina.

"Shouldn't let that stuff stay in the kitchen. I'll put her trash outside."

Ronald was gone nearly an hour. At some point, washing dishes, Mina looked through the kitchen window and saw a shadow, Ronald presumably, moving between the house and the trashcans lined up along the back alley. She was mending socks at the kitchen table when Ronald came up the basement stairs half an hour later.

"Well," he said, rubbing his hands. "Our neighbor has a secret life, wouldn't you know." He poured himself a cup of coffee from the Silex warming on the stove and sat down across from Mina. "She's a *poetess*, no less." He sneered.

"How do you know?" Mina asked, trying to sound nonchalant.

"She has poems, pages of poems, stacked on her desk."

"You saw her desk? She has a desk in the kitchen?"

"Of course not," Ronald snapped. "Upstairs. In her bedroom."

"You went into her bedroom?"

"And why oh why not? I had a look around while I was over there. No telling what they're doing—drugs, mojo. I considered it my civic duty." He smiled smugly.

Mina composed her face, not wishing to reveal shock. Though Ronald would not have noticed. Ronald rarely looked at her, even on those few occasions when they had sex.

But something, perhaps a sudden sharp release of breath, had betrayed her feelings.

"They're not like us," he insisted. "You can't treat them like us because they aren't *like* us. People like that"—he waved his hand dismissively—"those people live like animals."

The ensuing silence was ruptured suddenly by Baby's screams. Baby was hungry. Baby demanded to be fed. Ronald went upstairs to read.

Sunday was clear and bright; a light dusting of snow had fallen overnight. After breakfast Ronald set out for the library. Half an hour later Mina bundled Baby into her carriage, packing *Parade Magazine* and an issue of *Life* between the blankets for insulation, and set out for a long walk. Most of the students left on weekends. Townsfolk were scattered among the Lutheran, Baptist, and Episcopal congregations; others attended mass at St. Barnabas. Mina had the campus paths and the streets and sidewalks of the small town all to herself, and after church bells ceased their tolling no sounds disturbed the air. What sadness there is in such desertion, Mina thought, pushing Baby through the endless emptiness. And remembered last summer, on a bench in the tiny shaded park in Brooklyn, rocking Baby's carriage side by side with other new mothers, other educated women arrested by marriage and maternity. They had each other for chatter, commiseration, to laugh and cry with (often at once). Here was nothing.

A tear froze on her cheek.

Bells clanged, rudely intruding, as she approached First Baptist. Doors flew open and out poured streams of hearty worshippers, cleansed and uplifted, heading home to pork and chicken dinners, to lives of conviction and safety. A curious envy gnawed as she headed home.

Mina found Ronald in the kitchen. He was making coffee.

"Library was closed," he said. "Some dumb thing." Though he didn't seem displeased.

He had a sheaf of papers tucked under his arm.

"Some of her stuff isn't bad," said Ronald, waving the papers.

"You've been over there again?" Mina laid Baby back in her bassinet. *Mirabile dictu*, Baby remained asleep.

Ronald ignored the question, or perhaps not. "Not bad at all. With a little polishing, it might be published."

"You're going to help Dorothy get her poems published?"

"In a manner of speaking, yes."

Ronald headed upstairs, to copy Dorothy's poems he said. And then he'd put them back, the originals, before she got home.

Baby slept on. Grateful Mina laid out galleys and resumed proofreading. At one o'clock she delivered Ronald's grilled cheese sandwich to his office. The door was closed. She knocked.

"Just leave it there," said Ronald.

At four-thirty Mina interrupted her proofreading to make a meatloaf. Baby had now been asleep nearly five hours. Mina washed bits of chopped onion and grease from her hands and slid the pan and two large potatoes into the oven. Then she went to the alcove to have a look at Baby. Baby's face was pink. Mina touched her forehead. It felt warm, though perhaps that was because Mina's hands had been in the oven.

Mina resumed her proofreading. Half an hour later Ronald came hurriedly into the kitchen, clutching pages of typescript, and rushed down the basement stairs. And returned in a few moments, calmer.

"You needn't have hurried," said Mina, not looking up. "She doesn't come back till after supper."

"Dinner," Ronald corrected. "But better safe than sorry."

"How're you going to tell her?" Mina asked, pushing the galleys aside. "About getting her stuff published?" She stood up. "Planning to surprise her with a copy of *Poetry*?" Did she sound sarcastic? She hoped so.

"She'll never know," said Ronald.

And then Mina understood that Ronald intended to publish Dorothy's poems as his own.

When Baby remained asleep at six, despite assault by Beethoven on the kitchen radio and smells of roasting meat and potatoes, Mina decided that something was wrong. With trepidation she removed Baby's sodden diaper. Baby, hot as a stovepipe, didn't stir. Mina inserted the thermometer in her rectum. 102.8 degrees.

Mina called the doctor, a fat lame man with five daughters who lived on the other side of town. "Give her a sponge bath," the doctor barked. Children squabbled in the background. "It's Sunday night; I don't do house calls on Sunday."

She undressed Baby, laid her in the kitchen sink, and began sponging cool water over the flaccid torso and flopping limbs. Baby reminded her of the latex doll she'd gotten on her eighth birthday. *A present from the social worker who'd come out to her aunt's "to see how things are going." Who saw. And winced. Then frowned and sniffed. "You're not keeping the place clean," said the social worker to Mina's aunt. Mina was sent into the bedroom while the aunt and the social worker talked. The doll was cheap and wore only a diaper; it had no other clothes.*

Mina laid Baby on a towel she had spread on the drainboard. She opened Baby's eyelids with her thumb and saw glassy pools, slate-colored. Was Baby breathing? How could you tell? She placed fingertips lightly on Baby's thin chest and felt the faint pulsing of Baby's heart, or maybe her own trembling fingers. She dressed Baby hurriedly and wrapped her in the sateen-banded cot blanket. No time to get Ronald. Mina grabbed her coat and ran out to the car with Baby in her arms.

At the emergency room Mina had to wait in line, behind two teenage boys wheeled in from a car accident and a man who'd sawed off part of his thumb. ("Serves you right," said the nurse taking down the man's information. "Working on the Lord's day and all.") Mina found a seat near the soda machine. The chairs were orange and rigid, made of molded plastic with thin metal legs. Mina's arms ached from holding Baby but there was no place to lay her and Mina had left the carry cot in the car. No one seemed in any special hurry to help. After half an hour the teenage boys disappeared into a curtained cubicle. The man with the bloody thumb wrapped in a dirty handkerchief chatted with the nurse until he too was led away. Baby may be dead, thought Mina. And they will think I killed her.

"Next?"

Mina told the nurse her story, Baby's story. The nurse pressed a buzzer. Another nurse appeared and took Baby from Mina. "We'll just have a look." And walked off with her, leaving Mina behind.

"Should I . . . ?"

The nurse at the desk gave Mina a hard look. "Parents can be a bother," she said. "Best to wait here."

In the lobby Mina found a pay phone and called Ronald. The phone rang a dozen times before he answered. They had only one phone, on the kitchen wall by the sink.

"You really needed to go to the hospital?" said Ronald, after she'd explained. He sounded annoyed. No. Aggrieved. Ronald was usually aggrieved when his life was disrupted.

"Take out the meatloaf and potatoes," said Mina. "And turn off the oven."

"She's back," said Ronald. "I hear them on the porch. I'm going over now and tell her about the smell."

"I don't know how late I'll be," said Mina, and hung up.

The doctor who looked at Baby was thin, with the thinness of country people underfed as children. His face was splotchy, his thin sandy hair wasn't too clean. He spoke with the accent of the rural poor. Which befitted the place, thought Mina: the university was in a federally designated poverty area. Lyndon Johnson had even come to visit, and Bobby Kennedy was due to give a speech sometime in the spring.

The doctor came out to the waiting room to talk to Mina. He was carrying a clipboard.

"We got your little girl hooked up to an IV," the doctor said. He seemed to be addressing the wall behind her shoulder, but she couldn't be sure; his glasses were thick and smeared. "Running a high temp, higher'n we like to see. One-o-four-point-two." He paused, still looking at the wall, or maybe at Mina herself. "Gonna give her some anteebee-*ot*-ics soon as we get her hydrated." He dropped his head and the glasses slid slightly, unmasking his eyes. "Say, you don't seem too upset by all this, now do you?" he said. Mina realized that she had said nothing, could not in fact speak.

"How long you say she's been like this?" He fumbled with sheets pinned to the clipboard. Baby's records presumably. And then, ominously: "You know, I could report you."

"For what?" said Mina, and burst into tears.

The foster home where the social workers took Mina to live was clean and warm, and there was always enough to eat. She had her own room with a painted dresser and a pink crocheted bedspread and even a little desk in the corner where she could do her homework. Her foster parents were nice enough. Mr. and Mrs. George, she called them. Their last name was longer and unpronounceable. Mr. George sold insurance. Mrs. George was a homemaker who wore a frilly apron to do the housework and baked sugar cookies and made molded salads. Sometimes she let Mina press cinnamon hearts on the cookies, or decorate cups of cherry Jell-O with whipped Milnot and walnut halves. Once a month, on a Saturday afternoon, Mina's aunt came to see her. The two of them, Mina and her aunt, would walk into town and have sundaes at the Sweet Shop. Mina's aunt always asked her if she was happy, and Mina always said yes.

"Just let her be, let her be." Someone was patting her arm, an older woman, heavy-set, with permed iron-grey hair. "She just fainted is all. Bring her some water. It's awful hot in here."

"Well, I guess you'd know about as well as anyone," said another woman's voice. The nurse behind the desk. "Even though you haven't been around awhile."

"Now you don't forget your calling just like that, do you?" said the first woman, holding a paper cup of water to Mina's lips.

"You been on leave six months, Selma," said the desk nurse. "You fixing to come back soon?"

"Soon's I get my O.K. from the orthopod," said Selma. "Have an appointment tomorrow afternoon." She helped Mina back into the chair. "There you go. Easy does it, honey. . . . See?" she said to the nurse. "Back's just about where it should be. Though this little thing's light as a feather."

"And now that husband of yours gets himself in a real fix." The desk nurse said this with a chuckle.

"Lucky it wasn't his whole hand," said Selma. "Doctor says it ain't too bad. Just sawed off the tip. Thumb should heal up just fine." She looked at her watch. "Should be done sewing him up pretty soon. And then we can head home." She turned to Mina. "You be needing a ride somewhere, honey?"

Mina managed to say that she had a car.

"You're in no shape to drive. Can I give you a lift?"

"I have to stay here," said Mina.

"Her baby's real sick," said the desk nurse to Selma, rolling her eyes.

"Well, I'm sorry to hear that, dear," said Selma, patting Mina's hand. "You just take care—everything's going to be all right."

It was now ten o'clock. Mina had been at the hospital nearly four hours. At eight, directed by the nurse, she had gone downstairs to the basement cafeteria and paid fifty cents for a bowl of soup and a roll and a cup of cocoa. And lingered after finishing her meal, reluctant to return to the emergency room. She half wished that Ronald would come, felt relieved that he'd stayed away. She wondered whether he had talked to Dorothy. What he had said. Back upstairs, resettled in the molded plastic chair, she willed herself to thumb through the stack of tattered magazines. *Good Housekeepings* and *Ladies' Home Journals* mostly, articles on how to decorate your home, feed your family, save your marriage. Pages torn from an old *Life*, pictures of Jackie and the children at the funeral two years ago. A Spiderman comic book, orange crayon scribbles on the cover. Two issues of *National Geographic,* missing bits of features on the Amazon and Mauretania and the Dalai Lama's refuge in Dharamsala. But here was a spread, intact: the terra cotta soldiers found in China. She tried to count the figures, hundreds—thousands?—receding toward a brown horizon.

It was nearly eleven when the doctor, another one this time, came out to tell her that Baby—he called her Millie—was dead.

When Mina's parents were killed, her aunt got the call. Mina was staying over with her aunt, her mother's sister. It was a Saturday night. The driver who hit her parents' car said her parents were driving on the wrong side of the road. Whether this was true or not was never ascertained. The police chief's son was the other driver. Mina's father was unemployed and known to drink. Mina's mother, the police chief's daughter by a previous and unhappy marriage, was estranged from her father. Nolo contendere.

Mina remained with her aunt until she was taken to live with Mr. and Mrs. George. "A bright little thing," said the Georges. "Loves to read." Somewhere in her lineage, Mina had been told by her aunt, was a chief justice of the Massachusetts Supreme Court. That was on her father's side. And a Harvard professor (theology), and the man who invented adhesive tape, on her mother's. Brains, old brains had sired Mina. She had left at fourteen to go to boarding school—the police chief, perhaps conscience-stricken, had paid. And she had never returned.

There were papers to sign. "Your husband must also consent," said the woman in the business office. "To what?" said Mina. "That she's dead?"

The woman looked at her oddly. "To release the body for burial. Both parents must sign." She tapped a line on the form with a ballpoint pen.

"He's not here—he doesn't know," said Mina.

"Well, now," said the woman, reaching for the phone. "Perhaps," she suggested, and her voice was not unkind, "it's time to call him?"

"No, no—don't," said Mina.

"I don't mean telling him over the phone. But he has to come here. We can break the news . . . gently."

As if Ronald cares, thought Mina bitterly. But she took the phone and dialed, and eventually Ronald answered.

Baby had been dead for more than an hour when they led Mina in to see her. Septicemia is what they told her. A massive infection. These things happened. No, it was not her fault, and shame on that doctor for suggesting otherwise but she, Mina, should understand that poor Doctor Godfrey had been working for thirty-six hours straight. Tired people said things they shouldn't. "She's in shock, poor thing," the nurses whispered, explaining to themselves Mina's mute passivity. Mina bent over the waxy little body and kissed its cold forehead. She had seen someone do that in a movie years ago; that must be what you did when your baby died.

Ronald said they should have Baby cremated. It was cheaper than burial, and besides, these country funerals were tacky things, with undertakers soaking you for cheap coffins, not to mention headstones that crumbled in a thunderstorm.

"Arrangements can be made in the morning," said the woman in the business office, ignoring Ronald's execration of local custom. "Nobody's open now."

It was after one o'clock. Ronald had showered and shaved before taking a taxi to the hospital.

Mina drove them home. At the front door, as Mina slipped the key into the lock, Ronald reminded her that he had a seminar on Monday afternoon. "You'll have to handle this," he said.

Wednesday evening. Mina is checking the last galley for *Orchids: The Incredible Journey*. Ronald is having dinner at his adviser's house. Mina has not been invited. Hearing a noise, she looks up from the kitchen table and sees someone at the back door, a woman peering in through the glass, rapping lightly. Dorothy.

"I am just so sorry," says Dorothy, stepping into the kitchen. Dorothy has kind eyes and a sweet-sad smile. "I have just heard about your baby girl and I am so very very sorry." She extends both hands. "If there is anything . . . "

"How did you hear?" asks Mina, ignoring Dorothy's hands and moving toward the stove. She turns the gas flame high under the teakettle. "Would you like some tea?"

Dorothy, rejected, drops her hands. "No, no thank you. I can't stay. But I just wanted you to know—"

But Mina persists: "How did you hear? Who told you?"

"Why, it's in the paper," Dorothy replies, looking slightly surprised.

"An article?" says Mina, aghast.

"In the Deaths column—I'll clip it for you . . . if you'd like."

"No thank you," says Mina, reaching into the cupboard for teabags and cups.

"Well, again, if there's anything I can do . . ." Dorothy turns to leave.

"No, wait. Don't go yet. Please."

"You're working," says Dorothy, glancing at the galleys on the table. "I didn't mean to intrude."

"You're not. Intruding I mean." Mina pours water into two china cups, then drops a teabag in each.

"But I can't—"

"Please—just for a few minutes." Mina stacks the galleys at one end of the table, then hands Dorothy a cup and saucer and motions for her to sit. "Sugar? Milk? I'm sorry I don't have any—"

"No, nothing, thank you. I'll only stay a minute." Dorothy shrugs her mouton coat onto the back of the chair. She is neatly dressed, dressed for work in a navy suit and silky white blouse with a bow. Hose. Trim leather boots with small heels. Nails neatly manicured. Mina, sitting across from her in jeans and sweatshirt and bedroom slippers, realizes that she, Mina, has not bathed in three days. Or left the house since Monday, when she had to see to Baby's arrangements. That's what the man at the funeral home called them: *arrangements.*

Dorothy dunks the teabag several times and places it on the saucer. She takes a sip of tea, then composes herself, folding her hands in her lap. "While I'm here, I must apologize . . . ," she begins.

"For what?" Mina asks, and then remembers.

"For that chicken," Dorothy says. "It must have smelled something awful. Your husband told me he got rid of it, and I am most grateful."

Mina shakes her head. "Don't worry about it. Ronald's a bit of a fusser."

"Well, I still feel bad about it . . . especially now. I should have been a better neighbor." She takes another sip of tea, replacing the cup carefully in the saucer.

"We all have so little time, don't we," Mina says. "For leisure, I mean."

"That is certainly the case, isn't it." Dorothy glances at her watch.

"What do you do for relaxation?" Mina asks suddenly, impulsively.

"Me? Oh, I just like to read, I guess. The children keep me real busy, so getting the chance to read by myself is a treat." She smiles. "Of course that usually happens only at night, after they've gone to bed. Though I can read at work on my lunch hour sometimes, too."

"What sort of things do you like to read? Novels? Biography? History?"

"Oh, nothing too long," says Dorothy. "Poetry. That's what I like."

"Oh? What kinds?"

Dorothy beams. "Well, I like lots of poetry, but I guess I have a few favorites. Mostly American. Let's see: Frost, and Millay. Bishop. Williams—I really like William Carlos Williams. . . . *'Without invention nothing is well spaced . . .'* How that man found time to write poetry with all his doctoring is hard to imagine." She pauses. "You know," she confides, leaning forward, "English was always my favorite subject in school."

Mina takes one sip of tea, then another before speaking. "Ever tried writing poetry yourself?"

"Oh, my no—not since high school. But what I like to do is copy it out."

"Copy it?"

"You know—write it down in my own hand. Fixes it in my mind. That way I can memorize it." She looks at Mina. "It's a comfort," Dorothy says. "When times are bad I've got my comfort right here." She taps her forehead lightly. "You do that too?"

Mina fiddles with the teabag still soaking in her cup. "I used to," she says. "When I was a child. Old-fashioned things. We had to learn them in school."

"Well, there you are!" says Dorothy, and reaches out to pat Mina's hand. "And now I really must get back. Darwin's got a headache—always gets a headache when he has a math test coming up." She slips on her coat. "Thank you so kindly for the tea. And remember—if there's anything you need, we're right next door."

Nearly everything she owns has been packed. Five boxes of books and a steamer trunk have been delivered to the train station, driven there by Mina herself this morning, after Ronald left for the library; they will ship by railway freight. The rest of her things are in two suitcases, clothes mostly, plus the family silver, *her* family silver, bits and pieces of flatware passed down; her aunt gave them to her, a few days before she died. Her aunt who couldn't keep a clean house, her aunt who was too fond of cheap wine, who used to wonder aloud, when she'd come for visits—this was after Mina was grown and living in New York—used to wonder aloud, rhetorically, what had become of the family. "Once grand," she'd say. "Once so very grand." And then she'd look Mina straight in the eye: "But you, my girl, will save us!"

Baby's things, the carry cot and the bassinet and the carriage filled with a mound of tiny clothes, have been left on the front porch for the Salvation Army.

The galleys and manuscript for *Orchids: The Incredible Journey* have been delivered to the press; she dropped them off this morning, after her stop at the train station. She included a forwarding address, for her final check. She has also enclosed a note suggesting that before proceeding with publication the editor might wish to check Professor Llabbattarrya's manuscript against *Orchids: Their Provenance*, available at the university library.

The car is in her name. It should get her back. Or she can sell it along the way, and take the train.

She has left a letter for Ronald, a short one. It says that his mother's china, the odds and ends of chipped Rose Medallion bestowed upon them as a wedding present, is in the cupboard. It reminds him that the right rear gas burner does not ignite. It informs him that the last of his laundry is in the dryer. The argyle sox have gotten mixed in with the white boxers and undershirts—he will have to sort them out.

Queer

Betty, known as Miss Betty to her pupils, taught piano; Pearl helped around the house. They arrived in town in the late Thirties, before the war, before paved streets. "I knew right away this was my kind of place," said Betty for years afterward, to anyone who asked why she'd come. The accent, not New England, prompted the occasional query. New people mostly, mothers making pleasant conversation while their daughters and sometimes sons, though Betty preferred girl pupils, handed coats over to Pearl and smoothed out their sheet music. "Saw a fellow on a horse coming down the street, reminded me of home. Missouri, little town you never heard of."

Lessons were given in the front parlor, on Betty's Hardeman grand. She'd bought it in Boston and had it trucked up to New Hampshire, riding in the front seat with the driver to make sure he avoided ruts. Betty had her diploma from Stephens College framed on the parlor wall. Above it hung a certificate that read "College of Music" but pupils could not read the fine print giving details. Mothers seldom went into the front parlor to see for themselves.

In fact the house and not a horse had drawn Betty to town. Willed to her by a great-uncle. Betty and Pearl came east to take up residence in 1937. May 13, 1937, to be exact. The day after Coronation Day. A framed, yellowed page from a local paper hung in the foyer, above the bench where the mothers of the youngest pupils sat and crocheted or did embroidery while their children stumbled through "Für Elise" on the Hardeman. GEORGE VI CROWNED, said the headline; LOCAL CEREMONIES COMMEMORATE GREAT EVENT. A large picture covered half the page, showing a man on horseback leading a parade. The man carried American and British flags. The town, a Tory stronghold in the Revolution, had retained its Anglo sympathies. This, it was assumed, was Betty's recollection of a horse.

Pearl was thought to be slow, as they used to say when they really meant retarded. She didn't talk much in the foyer, taking coats from Betty's pupils before disappearing into the rear of the house, or at the A&P, where she went every day, market basket over one arm, to buy the sorts of things that two older women needed to sustain their lives: half a loaf of bread, canned peas, sometimes an orange or two, chops or a piece of fish. (Staples—rice, potatoes, coffee—were bought in bulk and delivered by the grocer's boy.) Nor did Pearl say much at the Congregational church, where Betty played the organ for Sunday services. Sitting in a back pew, wearing a mink hat dulled by age and neglect, and a long black coat she never removed, Pearl remained silent for the Lord's Prayer and never sang the hymns.

Pearl was taller than Betty, by at least half a foot. This meant tall in its own right, as Betty was of average height. Pearl seemed to want to shrink herself. With Betty or alone, she walked down the street pitched forward, as if she were ducking the sky, or heading into a strong wind. Her head was always covered: In winter, by the mink hat; otherwise by various mouse-colored scarves tied over her head, peasant-style. This was outside as well as indoors, year-round. Her hair must have been close-cropped; you couldn't see much of it under the hat or scarves, and people didn't know what the color was, though they assumed grey, like Betty's. Pearl's face was lined and loose, implying age, or a hard life. Betty's was firmer, and the color changed according to the season; in winter she had freckles, concealed in summer by the tan she got from weeding the garden. The youngest Peterson boy mowed the grass; a succession of Petersons had tended the yard since anyone could remember.

Occasionally, when people had nothing else to talk about, they wondered what kept Betty and Pearl together, or what had brought them together in the first place, cheerfully earnest Betty, Pearl the long-faced mope. People who remembered when they first came had died or moved away or were now, twenty years on, too old to remember or care.

Betty and Pearl were town fixtures, as inseparable from their yellow house on Main Street as they were from each other.

Half a century ago, in a small New England town, someone was said to be queer who was more than a bit peculiar, nothing else. It didn't mean sex. Of the two, Pearl was peculiar going on queer; Betty, ardent church member, generous donor to the policemen's benevolent fund, helpful neighbor to the arthritic Donaldson brothers next door, was neither; she fit right in, like a married lady. Though Betty was a spinster, like Miss Simms the lame schoolteacher who lived with her mother a few doors down, and Edwina Perkimer, who sold stamps and money orders in the post office and wore a fresh, flouncy handkerchief, one for each day of the year, in the breast pocket of her smock. The men said maiden ladies were peculiar because they had no man to take care of; women, married women, didn't comment. Betty, the men said, could have got herself a husband if she wanted, made a good wife, what with all her energy. Planted marigolds and dusty miller in the front yard in spring, dished up strawberry sundaes at the church ice cream social each June, made her famous scalloped potatoes for the volunteer firemen's lobster fest on Labor Day weekend. Betty, with iron-gray plaits coiled around her head and sensible glasses, the kind without fancy frames, and neat plain dresses in dark wool or pastel cotton, depending on the season—Betty, everyone said, was as regular as the weather. Betty fit in. She lived openly, exposed, without secrets. Pearl, by contrast, seemed folded inside herself, revealing nothing. But most folks assumed she had nothing to reveal. That made her acceptable; undeniably peculiar going on queer, but acceptable.

The fuss started innocently enough, with a letter. It was registered. Betty had to go to the post office to sign for it because she'd been helping down at the church the day before, when the mailman came. Pearl was out at the A&P, for which, in retrospect, Betty was grateful. Edwina Perkimer, filling in for the postmaster, handed over the letter. Betty commented pleasantly on Edwina's handkerchief, a gauzy sky blue number spotted with white polka dots, but Edwina merely gave her usual sniff and called "Next."

In the vestibule Betty adjusted her glasses to read the dim postmark: Maniteo, Missouri. She looked at the return address and recognized it. She slipped the letter into her brown leather pocketbook, snapped it shut, and headed to the library.

Betty went to the library when she wanted privacy. An observant woman, she knew its shapes and shadows by heart: a pile of grey-tan boulders, worn smooth by rain and sleet and roofed with weathered cedar shakes, nesting snugly among tall conifers and clumps of wavy, overgrown ferns. Inside, a warren of dimly lit, closet-like anterooms housed sagging shelves of faded books, torn magazines, yellowed newspapers. In the lounge off the entrance foyer, Stickley chairs upholstered in worn brown leather faced a massive stone fireplace where gas logs now flickered year round.

Betty had begun making the library her refuge soon after her arrival. More people used the library back then, and when she wanted to be alone she had to perch in a window seat in one of the anterooms, usually the one that shelved science and philosophy. Hardly anyone went there, the fiction room and the current-magazine nook being the most popular. Today, however, no one was in the lounge, and old Mrs. Fogerty the librarian, who had a large wart protruding through thin grey hair on top of her head and wasn't sociable, was busy behind the desk and didn't look up when she walked in.

Betty settled herself in one of the Stickley chairs near the window, where no one could come up behind her, or advance sideways, to see what she was doing. She pulled out the letter, typed on an old manual by the looks of it, jumpy letters unevenly printed, some dark, some faded where the key had struck a worn spot on the ribbon.

> *My dear Elizabeth Ellen,*
>
> *I hope this finds you well and happy. I always wished nothing but happiness for you, you know that, at least I hope you do.*

(Betty took note of the run-on sentence and read on.)

> *And so I have tracked you down at last! This thanks to your cousin Wilfrid, who I saw on the TV when all that*

Sputnik business was going on. They were interviewing him on the evening news, and I said to myself that is Elizabeth Ellen's cousin Wilfrid, he was always so smart and now look where those brains have got him—on national TV, imagine that! Anyway, I called information in Alabama, that's where the TV man said he was teaching, and I got his number.

Don't worry, I didn't tell him anything, I just said I was an old friend of Elizabeth Ellen's from home and did he have your address? He was a little bit impatient, I guess he's a busy man isn't he, but he told me you were up someplace in New England, and as they say the rest is history!! It took awhile but this country is not as big as some people think. People can't run off and hide the way they used to.

Elizabeth Ellen, you were a naughty girl to do what you did all those years ago but I bear no grudges. However, we are getting on in years, you and I, and while the past is past don't you think it's time we put things right? With a great big hug if nothing else? Well I think so and I intend to do something about it. I am coming east soon. Please don't go away again. I want to see you, and you can't run away anymore. As the song says, I'll come knockin' on your door! Meanwhile, if you feel like writing me you know where to send the letter. I haven't moved.

Dearest love,
Your Tibby

P.S. You will notice I have not mentioned Pearl. I did not want to get you upset ahead of time.

Betty must have sighed, or groaned. She heard a tremulous "Is everything all right?" Mrs. Fogerty bent over her. The pulsing wart, pink as the slick lumps of Dubl Bubbl her pupils stuck furtively under the piano, suggested agitation. Betty folded the letter and tucked it back in her purse. She tried to smile. "Nothing to be concerned about. Just some family business."

Which Mrs. Fogerty thought was probably untrue. Everybody in town knew that Betty had received a registered letter from Missouri. Concern was there all right.

Betty carried on, giving no sign of weakness or possible breakdown. With Pearl, with pupils, at church, with the Donaldson brothers she was her usual cheerful, helpful self. She tipped Frankie Peterson an extra nickel when he cut the lawn. At the A&P she made a point of seeking out Mrs. Fogerty in the produce aisle and asking after her cats. She betrayed no concern at the Meet 'n' Eat Café when she joined some of the church widows for Sunday lunch (Pearl went straight home after the service). Talk in town about the letter slowly faded. Perhaps it had been only family business after all, an estate settlement maybe, news of a pending sale of land. Still, no one was aware that Betty had any family left. She never went back to Missouri, as far as anyone knew, and no one came to visit. But people didn't pry. If Betty needed their help, she'd get it. But they'd wait till she asked.

A Thursday morning, nearly noon, in late May, three weeks after the letter arrived, by which time Betty had almost succeeded in putting Tibby out of her mind. Betty was out in the front yard tidying up the forsythia with a pair of ancient hedge clippers nearly as long as her arms. Memorial Day was tomorrow, the parade would go right by their house. "Want the place looking good," she said by way of greeting Mr. Moser, the mailman. Mr. Moser ignored this. "Got another one of them letters," he said, reaching in his brown pouch for a pen. "Just sign here." He pointed to a line on the Registered Mail receipt hanging from the envelope.

She couldn't get dressed up right then and there and go to the library. Besides, she remembered, it was closing at noon, for the long weekend. Feeling tired and weak, she crept slowly around the side of the house, to a worn stone bench under the copper beech shading much of the backyard. She hoped Pearl was busy with her dusting inside, or was this Pearl's day to do the mending? She couldn't remember. *Let Pearl be,* she prayed silently, and opened the letter.

She had already seen the postmark—*Maniteo, Mo.* And her name and address in the same jumpy type, the letters all in caps.

> *Dearest Elizabeth Ellen,*
>
> *This is to inform you I will be arriving Thurs. May 29. Sometime in the afternoon I think though don't hold me to it. I'm driving a long ways to see you but the car is in good shape and my driving is much improved over what you may remember, ha ha! Don't go to any special trouble about dinner or anything. This will be my treat. We can go out in my car. You have a place to eat in that little town, I'm sure of it.*

(Betty looked at the postmark again: May 25. Before the war she and Pearl had made the trip in a week. But the roads hadn't been as good back then.)

> *You have not written me and maybe that is because of the shock you have received from hearing from me after all these years. I was hoping you'd tell me something about Pearl though I did not want to go into details in my first letter because I do not want you to think I harbor any bitterness about the situation. Is she still with you? If so, she can come out to eat with us. Meanwhile, see you soon!*
>
> *Dearest love,*
>
> *Your Tibby*

She was coming after all.

A restaurant. The Meet 'n' Eat? Out of the question. Loud Tibby, with her bleached hair, she assumed she still bleached her hair, or maybe did something else outlandish with it, and her bright clothes and what she called her "dramatic" costume jewelry that left green rings on her neck and fingers. Though she was older now. Maybe she'd toned down some, improved her taste, though there was no telling. Tibby had money, way back when, family money despite the Depression. Her daddy had been the town banker. Some folks wondered why he hadn't gone under when the rest of Maniteo did, but they kept their mouths shut. Had she been through it all, spending on gewgaws and hairdressers and two-piece floozy dresses with dyed-to-match hats and shoes? But she must have had some left. Driving across half the country wasn't cheap, and Tibby wasn't the sort of person who'd sleep in her car.

Why was she coming anyhow? To reconcile, that's what the first letter said. Betty had hoped, dreamed, prayed she wouldn't carry out her plan. And now here she was. Would be. Sometime in the next few hours.

Pearl was polishing silver in the kitchen. A set of Revere flatware, left to Betty along with the house. They only used it Christmas and Easter, and once a year in September when Betty had the minister and his wife over to tea. Did Pearl sense a visitor coming?

"Your four o'clock canceled," said Pearl, not looking up. "Sore throat."

"Just as well," said Betty. The annoying little Streator girl, who arrived each week with fingers sticky from licorice whips she bought coming home from school.

Pearl always kept herself occupied. That was a relief at least. Polishing didn't hurt the silver.

"You going back out with those shears?"

Betty was still holding the hedge clippers. The letter was tucked in her apron pocket. "We have to talk, Pearl," she said. "Go wash your hands now; you can finish up the silver later."

When a black Buick with what Betty thought was excessive chrome trim pulled into the drive at four o'clock sharp, Betty and Pearl were waiting in the front parlor, seated adjacently, facing outward, on the piano bench. This position commanded the best view of the driveway. They wore their summer church dresses, Betty's a green rayon print, Pearl in a sky blue dotted swiss with a white piqué collar. The collar was detachable; Pearl laundered it separately every week, on Sunday evening. Both of them wore white gloves, and Betty had found one of her own straw hats with a wide brim to fit Pearl, thinking it more suitable than Pearl's usual head scarf.

Through a side window dressed with lace curtains, what the salesgirl in Portsmouth years ago had called "demi-sheer," Betty watched a large female person climb rather stiffly from the car. The female person, Betty noted with some relief, was wearing a two-piece navy dress with white trim. The female person's blond hair was subdued, probably by a net. No hat, Betty noted with silent disapproval, though she quickly reminded herself that this was far better than she could have hoped for.

When the front bell rang a few minutes later, Betty and Pearl were by the door, waiting.

How much should she tell Pearl? How much did Pearl remember? Pearl was slow, of course, but Pearl could surprise you with what she knew, what she'd picked up from watching instead of talking most of her life. Pearl had been twenty or thereabouts when they'd come east; Betty was already in the next decade, early thirties to be sure but still the next decade. There was a world of difference, Betty felt, between twenties and thirties. But the point was this: Pearl had been old enough to remember.

A few hours earlier, she'd asked Pearl to follow her into the back parlor, the one they used every day, the front parlor being overtaken by the piano. And when Pearl had sat down and folded her hands and waited to be told what to do next, Betty began talking about their big trip a long time ago, the one on the long silver bus with the giant running dog painted on the side. And Pearl had nodded when, at carefully spaced intervals, Betty would ask "Do you remember?" Of course, a sign of assent did not necessarily mean that Pearl understood, but it did suggest that Pearl was not baffled or distressed by Betty's narrative.

"And we carried a big suitcase between us, *do you remember?"*

Yes, nodded Pearl, yes, she remembered. She remembered it all.

Now, sitting in the back parlor with the large female person, Pearl did not seem confused or dismayed, even when the large female person kept patting her arm and reaching out to squeeze her hand. The hand was wearing lots of heavy rings with sharp colored stones that hurt Pearl but she didn't cry out. She just sat silently, looking ahead.

Even when Betty said to her, as gently as she could, "Pearl, Tibby's your aunt, your mama's sister. She's come to see you."

Even when Tibby, forceful, relentless, she hadn't changed, said to Betty, "I want to take her home."

"I can fix something here," said Betty, looking at her watch. It was nearly five o'clock. They, or rather Tibby, had been chatting away the better part of two hours in the back parlor. Stories about people back home, how they'd made out. Poor as church mice, the Depression to thank for that, but then the war came, the army built a parachute factory in town, things got better for most people. In the midst of a monologue on the third of Tibby's four husbands Betty served iced tea and thin sugar cookies with pink icing.

"Wouldn't dream of it," said Tibby, helping herself to the last cookie. "I see you've got a place up the road. My treat. Daddy left me all his money after all!" She grinned at Betty. "You remember—always said I wouldn't get a dime after he was gone, the way I liked to spend spend spend. Said it was going to the Legion for a new hall, but then he got mad at—." Tibby was off and running on another tale but Betty stopped her.

"Let's go now then," she said. Before the usual evening crowd came in.

The Meet 'n' Eat had only a few customers, two men in overalls and feed caps sitting at the counter drinking coffee and eating pie. Betty was happy to realize she didn't know them; truckers probably, taking a detour on their way home. Betty led Tibby and Pearl to a booth at the rear. Pearl ordered a double chocolate milk shake. "Ha, got your mother's sweet tooth," said Tibby, reaching across the table to pat her arm. "But you have to eat something else, too, honey." Pearl ignored this.

Betty and Tibby both asked for the special, fish platters. Tibby said she'd share hers with Pearl. Pearl shook her head and chewed her straw. The waitress was new and not a local; another relief for Betty. She allowed herself to relax a little and stirred extra sugar into her iced tea while they waited for the food to come. Tibby fumbled in her purse and drew out a folded white envelope.

"Brought you something, honey," she said, offering the envelope to Pearl. But Pearl wouldn't take it.

"C'm'on, it's for you. It belonged to your mama."

Pearl looked like she was going to cry. She sucked noisily on the straw, screwing up her face to block tears.

"I've told her . . . ," Betty began in a warning tone.

"I'm just trying to give her a little present, for pity's sake," said Tibby. "What's the harm in that?"

The fish platters arrived before Betty had to reply.

They ate without conversation for twenty minutes. Pearl had another milkshake and took several bites of Betty's coleslaw. She kept on ignoring Tibby. Tibby ate with determination but she was getting angry, steamed up they used to call it back home. Betty could tell, remembering the signs: flushed face, heavy breathing, an irritating little habit of stopping every minute to adjust her earrings. They looked like real amethysts. Betty wondered if one of the husbands had given them to her.

The envelope lay on the table.

Finished at last, Tibby put down her fork, dabbed at her lips with a paper napkin, and picked up the envelope. "It's a necklace, a locket. For you," she said, waving it in Pearl's face.

You didn't, Betty was about to say, but caught herself.

Minna lay in her coffin in an aquamarine evening dress, chiffon it must have been, real silk, rayon and nylon not being available back then. "He always treated her better than me," Tibby said. "And now will you look at that." She threw up her hands. "What a waste." Everyone must have heard, all the people who were friends of Daddy's and Minna's and a few of Tibby's, too. Minna was older, by nearly fifteen years. The child of Daddy's first marriage to The Most Wonderful Woman in the World, the One Who Died. The second marriage wasn't happy. In fact, it had been a disaster. A cocktail waitress from St. Joe's who'd run off soon after delivering Tibby. Minna and Daddy had raised her. Minna grew up but she stayed on, keeping house for Daddy and teenage Tibby. There were boyfriends from time to time, but Daddy didn't approve. You're a beauty, Daddy told her, better than all those fellas; don't waste yourself. In her late twenties Minna decided to have some fun. She eloped with one of those barnstorming boys who showed off at county fairs and the like, looping-the-loop in wispy mothlike planes that seemed lighter than air. But weren't. He crashed into a hayrick when Minna was six months pregnant. She saw it happen, the whole thing, the graceful ascent, the sudden plunge, the column of hot orange fire shooting straight up with a *whoosh* into the sky. It did something to her, people said, she wasn't the same after that. It did something to Pearl, too, at least that's what people blamed it on. A few months after Pearl was born, Minna, back home with Daddy, got hold of some chloroform from the druggist. She was going to use it on Pearl, some people said, but at the last minute she had a change of heart.

Betty idolized Minna. She became Tibby's friend afterwards.

"Is that Minna's locket?" Betty pointed at the envelope.

"You are positively clairvoyant," said Tibby.

Minna lay in her coffin in the aquamarine chiffon dress. Her blond head rested on a white silk pillow trimmed with Dresden lace. Manicured hands, nails slick with clear polish, clasped a pale pink lily. Her only jewelry besides a wedding ring was the gold locket, Daddy's present for her sixteenth birthday. It hung from a thin gold chain and had a small ruby in the center, Minna's birthstone.

The minister was saying final prayers. The undertaker stood by, waiting to close the coffin. Tibby and Betty were in back, behind the aunts and uncles and cousins and Daddy, who was blubbering into a large white silk handkerchief edged in black. Tibby pinched Betty. "When I yell, you go hide, hear?" she whispered.

And then Tibby screamed "FIRE!" at the top of her lungs.

"The one you s-t-o-l-e," said Betty. From a coffin, no less.

"Didn't," said Tibby. "It was rightfully mine." The waitress had brought her a slice of cherry pie. "You want some?" she said to Pearl, pushing the plate over. Pearl said nothing.

"I saw you," said Betty.

"Now you don't want to go starting something here, do you?"

Customers, regulars, were coming in now, filling up the booths and tables. What was the point?

But Tibby was a bulldozer. You had to stand your ground. As she herself had done twenty years ago. Packing herself and Pearl up in a big suitcase, diplomas wrapped in underwear and tucked between her aunt's cashmere shawl and the scrap of pink crib blanket that was all Pearl had of her babyhood. She carried the things they valued most or needed for the trip; the rest were sent ahead in a wardrobe trunk, shipped railway freight. Just when she'd thought there was no way out, the great-uncle had died and left her his house, half a continent away.

Betty signaled for the check. Tibby put the envelope in her purse.

Back in the car, Betty decided that matters had to be settled right then and there. They could have walked to the Meet 'n' Eat, it wasn't far, but she'd allowed Tibby to take them in the Buick

"Let's go for a drive, shall we," said Tibby. "My, my, look at all those flags."

Biding her time, Betty thought.

Tibby steered the car down Main Street, then turned left on Elm. They passed the Sinclair station, the outpost it was called, the last stopping place before town made way for country. Pearl was in the backseat. "Thought I saw a park around here, coming in this afternoon."

"The quarry," said Betty. "Make the second right. Miller Road."

The sun was going down ahead of them. Patches of fading light flickered through the trees.

"I could make trouble, you know," Tibby said. Her thick pink jeweled hands tightened on the steering wheel. "She's my blood relative."

"You didn't take care of her. That was your job, taking care of her. That's why your daddy let you spend his money, so you'd take care of her. And him, when he got sick. And you didn't do it."

"Ha, ha, ha. And what would you know about taking care of anyone? Who do you think took care of you? You had no family, not counting that woman who said she was your aunt and wasn't. Daddy paid for your college, for music school, out of the kindness of his heart."

And because he'd fleeced my aunt out of her savings and didn't want to go to jail, thought Betty, but said nothing.

"Nobody did that for me, oh no, Tibby was supposed to stay home just like Minna."

"I was smart," said Betty. "I did well in school. You liked boys."

"Come to think of it," said Tibby, "we *were* sort of a queer twosome, weren't we?"

A sign with an arrow, *Park Entrance/Closes at Sunset,* appeared. She turned into a weedy driveway sprinkled with gravel, drove a few yards, and shut off the engine.

"Guess this is as good as anyplace, wouldn't you say?"

"Pearl," said Betty, "you go take a walk now, okay? You know this place, we come here for picnics, remember? Go on over by the swings. We'll be there in a few minutes."

"She stays here," said Tibby, reaching back to lock the door, but Pearl had sprung out of the car and was heading down the path. In the right direction, Betty noted.

"Well, now," said Tibby, leaning back. She was thick across the bustline; pearl buttons strained against dark blue cloth, threatened to come undone, or snap off. "So this is how you take care of her? Letting her run out there?"

"She knows where she is. She'll be fine."

"I suppose you don't have rapists around here, axe murderers."

"There's a guard by the playground. He stays till dusk."

"Which it's getting to be now, in case you haven't noticed."

"So let's be brief: What do you want?"

"What I said before: to take her back with me."

"She's happy here."

"Happy?" Tibby snorted. "She's a half-wit. She doesn't know happy. Or sad or anything else."

"She's happy," Betty said, refusing to amend. "She has a home. Things to do. A life."

"You ran off with her, kidnapped her. You had no right."

"So why didn't you do something? Because you were drinking too much to notice. Drinking too much to see you needed her to cook and wash and iron and wait on your daddy. Any way he wanted."

Tibby suddenly raised a hand, maybe to slap, but didn't. The hand paused for an instant, in midair, then dropped into her lap. "You're a fine one to talk. You had no daddy, everybody knew that, no daddy to talk about." But the taunt had no sting. Tibby was crying.

Betty let her be for a few minutes. Then, as gently as she could, she said, "We're getting to be old women now, look at us." She wanted to stroke Tibby's plump hand, bring it to her cheek, the way her aunt had done when she was troubled. But could not.

Wouldn't. So sat instead in silence, looking into near darkness. Fireflies flashed in the purplish air. Up ahead, two figures walked slowly toward the car, one tall, the other short and thick.

"Miz Betty, that you?" called a male voice. Pearl with Jimmy, the child-man who guarded the playground.

Betty was up early the next morning. The marchers would pass her house, on the way to the cemetery. She would serve them lemonade, as she and the other church ladies along the route had done for years. She never went to the cemetery herself, though the great-uncle was buried there. The marchers, most of them old men, would put flowers and tiny flags on all the soldiers' graves. The great-uncle had been a soldier, a little boy soldier, in the Civil War.

After a quick cup of tea she got the juicer from the cupboard and lemons from the old Kelvinator. And wondered, as she sliced and squeezed and poured, when Tibby would awaken. Tibby had spent the night, at Betty's invitation. But first she had cried, a long therapeutic cry, in the back parlor, and then, still heaving, she had hugged Betty, and then Pearl, who looked mystified but allowed herself to be drawn stiffly to Tibby's damp bosom. And finally, fortified by medicinal brandy, Tibby had been tucked into a trundle bed in the spare room.

But it was Pearl who came into the kitchen, a few minutes after seven. She had her Sunday dress on, the dotted swiss with detachable collar, and she wore the straw hat Betty had given her the day before.

"Well, don't you look nice," said Betty, handing her a cup of tea, and then she noticed something else. Hanging around Pearl's neck, almost swallowed up in the loose folds of the dress, was a gold locket with a ruby stuck in the center.

"She gave it to me," said Pearl, touching the locket. "Said I should wear it."

Betty leaned out the side window. Tibby's car was gone.

"That was all?" Betty asked.

"It belonged to Mama," said Pearl. "There doesn't have to be anything else." She carried her tea out to the front porch, settled herself on the second step, and waited for the parade to begin.

Remains

The gloves were still there today. Smooth leather, dyed bright blue, trimmed in matching dyed-blue fur. Lying a few yards apart on the trackbed, crumpled and splotched with slush and whatever else falls from trains. Once upon a time human waste spilled on the tracks, but I guess that doesn't happen anymore. And not on a local train line. I don't think the trains here have toilets. I haven't noticed any, and I've been riding back and forth to the city for five years. The gloves were expensive, once. But not worth much now, I suppose. Though they could still keep someone warm.

But no one wants a dead person's gloves, do they?

You have to wonder about the kind of person who could do a thing like that. Granted, the day was dreary. Grey rain. Cold. So a person who's depressed anyway might think, Why not? There being no good reason in that person's mind to wait for the day and the mood to pass, for sun, for spring. I have felt that way, too, sometimes. But I would never ever end my life in a violent way. A plastic bag is better; it causes the least upset. You have to think of who's going to find you, after all.

I guess she was pretty mangled. Maybe the gloves have her bloodstains on them. I couldn't get close enough to see. Other people are always around, waiting for the next train. I think everybody knows who the gloves belong, or belonged, to. This is a small town. But we all avert our eyes. The platform is right by the tracks, on the same level. It would be so easy to just step over and take the gloves. But people are watching. They don't seem to be, but I know they are.

This is a small town. People notice.

Who would be called if I did such a thing?

She put notes, the newspaper said, in her boots and her pockets. The notes, said the newspaper, gave her husband's name and telephone number. Nothing else. I would not know what name, what number to give.

They must be her gloves. The newspaper said she was wearing a bright blue coat. The gloves must have matched. People would have noticed her, would have seen her before she did it; that's why they mentioned the coat, to help the police.

Her husband rides the train to work. Perhaps he will come by, at night maybe, to get the gloves.

I went into the city later this morning, just so I could take the same train. The train that killed her. The gloves hadn't been moved, as far as I could tell. It's been a week now. Perhaps I'm only imagining it, but the fingers seem to be curling slowly, the way fall leaves do when you bring them inside, hoping their colors will last. It may snow tonight, the radio said. It's November. Time for snow.

No one else was on the platform. I could have stepped over and taken the gloves and put them in the large tote bag I always carry to work. But I didn't. Someone might have seen me. You never know.

According to police, the engineer reported that she was curled up in the middle of the tracks. At first he did not know what was on the tracks, he said. He could only make out a bright blue object. He could not stop in time, he said. He has not been charged.

I have thought about writing to the engineer. A letter of apology. Anonymous, of course. Saying how sorry I am on her behalf for ruining his life. For his life *is* ruined, wouldn't you think? He has killed a woman, a young woman barely thirty. He has a daughter, the newspaper said. A daughter about the same age. He is grief-stricken, said the newspaper, and cannot return to work.

But perhaps the letter of apology should be coming from someone else. The husband, for instance.

The husband is key here, I do believe.

I would say that the husband should be looked at more closely. Wouldn't you?

Why hasn't he come for the gloves?

pretty mangled Why on earth would I write that, given my calling? I also noticed, in reading back over what I have written so far, that in the second paragraph I have committed a serious pronoun-agreement error. Sentence fragments are another thing altogether. Permissible these days.

But *pretty mangled* is a sly oxymoron, is it not? She was pretty. The newspaper said so. And she was mangled by the train. How did the gloves escape? Perhaps she removed them beforehand.

There is no excuse for pronoun-agreement error, except the rather weak one that colloquial usage is easier on the ear than stilted grammatical English. But that is something I have to watch out for. Talking within myself, converting thoughts into streams of speech. Mr. S, who runs our department, says I have lately not been up to my usual standards. Last week, on the very day that I first saw the gloves, he called me into his office to point out that the singular of *ova* is *ovum*. The manuscript was rather dull, a monograph on fruit fly mating in the Seychelles. And today, after I arrived at work two hours late, I was called in again. Told I was becoming increasingly indifferent to my duties. In what way, I asked. I have always had a streak of belligerence. There is only so much managing and manipulation that I will put up with. They are lucky to have me, after all.

I reminded Mr. S that I had told him the day before about being late for work this morning. My cat had to be taken to the vet, I said. I have no cat, but claiming ownership of a pet can be useful. If you live entirely alone, people think you're odd. And I have no relatives with convenient illnesses. The cat gives me an air of marginal normalcy and provides excuses when I wish to be absent from work. His name is Lancelot. He's a black-and-white tabby of uncertain age. I have a picture of him on my desk, clipped from a discarded *Cat Fancy* magazine I found at the Laundromat.

I told Mr. S that I would try to be more careful. I need the job, after all. Yes, they are lucky to have me, with my doctorate in Egyptian epigraphy, but truth to tell, no one else is going to hire me. I am fifty-two and could pass for sixty. People don't like to have elderly women around. What I want to know, though, is this: When we all die finally, those of us who have done this fool's job for years and years, checking spelling and grammar and dates and obscure facts about fruit flies and permafrost and the Thirty Years' War, who will be there to replace us?

The professor was right; I would never have made a good teacher. And I was dismal in the field, worried about snakes and third-world sanitation and dust that might aggravate my asthma. Work for a scholarly press, he said, meaning, I suppose, that I might hope to become the editor-in-chief one day. But my expertise was too narrow. Not many books are published on Twelfth Dynasty tomb inscriptions. One-time mistress of a single body of knowledge, I became a Jill-of-all-fields, certain only of my ability to determine the most reliable reference books for the current manuscript-at-hand.

Today I came home after dark, having stayed an extra hour to placate Mr. S. The fruit fly monograph is now on his desk for final review.

I have had my supper: a coddled egg and a piece of Rye-Vita and a pot of Earl Grey caffeine-free tea. And now I am going to open my tote bag, the one with a silk-screened picture of a tabby cat that I carry to work and back each day. Inside is the day's *Times* crossword, saved from lunch, and a new manuscript on Etruscan jewelry. Not really my line, but Mr. E, the other copy editor in the office, has his hands full with a botany encyclopedia at the moment. I told Mr. S I would have a look at it this evening.

I am saving the best for last. When I have finished the crossword and spent an hour or so with Etruscan goldsmiths, I will take out the last items in the tote bag. The blue, fur-trimmed gloves. I picked them off the tracks this evening. It was dark, but I could see them in the moonlight. No one was around. I put them in a plastic Fairway bag I had saved in the office for emergencies and tucked into my tote before leaving this evening.

I knew the gloves would still be there.

I do not live in the city because I want neighbors. Real neighbors, people you see every day and say hello to, not anonymous noises in the next apartment who hove into view only in an emergency, when the EMTs have to be called, or the undertaker. That happened several times on West Tenth, where I used to live. Never saw the people next door, or above me, till they came out in stretchers, taking me by surprise when I was leaving for work, or coming home of an evening. One, I recall, was in a green body bag, stabbed, the super said, by a jealous lover. He played strange music every evening, and the hall often smelled of what I am told is marijuana. I wouldn't know; I missed all that drug business somehow. In Egypt they smoked what I believe was hashish, but I didn't care to. I always had my work to keep me occupied.

I have a small house, but it suits me. I live on a quiet street of similar small houses. I know my neighbors, and they seem to know me. We nod or wave, going to and fro. There are bigger houses in other parts of this town, up on the hill, but my tiny bungalow suits me. I assume my house looks like every other house on the street, inside. Though I wouldn't know. I have never been inside the other houses.

Michael D lives in one of the bigger houses. He lived there with his wife, until it happened. Her name was Dora K. She kept her own family surname, apparently. Dora is an unusual name for a young woman today. They had no children, and that, as they say, is no doubt a blessing. Their house was—is—big. Perhaps they had planned on children. She was young, after all; he appeared—appears—somewhat older. Such a pretty girl, Dora. She rode my usual train home more often than not. Blue, bright blue, became her.

That last week, the day before it happened, she was crying on the evening train. She tried to hide it, hunched over in her puffy down coat, leaning toward the dark window, her elbow resting on the sill, her chin propped, awkwardly I thought, on a blue-gloved hand. But I saw.

Michael D never rode my train. I believe he works out here somewhere, not in the city. They moved to the house up the hill last spring. On my Saturday walks I would often see them, working in the yard. We never spoke; they were occupied with their planting, watering, mowing, raking.

I am an invisible woman, more so as I grow older. I have known that about myself for many years. If I did not raise my hand to wave at the neighbors on my own street, I doubt they'd notice me.

I saw Michael D at the newspaper store by the station this morning, buying a *Times* and a cup of coffee. While I was waiting in line he paid the cashier and left. He drove off in a white Toyota sedan, almost new. That is not the same car that sat in his driveway on weekends, a dark green Volvo wagon.

Be precise: he did not *drive* off, he *rode* off. Someone else was at the wheel. A woman.

The local paper has said nothing more about the incident. It is now three weeks since it happened.

They were stained with rain and soot, not blood. I've sponged off the dirt and they look quite nice, quite *presentable*, as my mother might have said. My mother favored such words. After only a moment's hesitation I tried them on and find they're a perfect fit. They look quite *smart*, another of Mother's favorites. The silky fur trim is a filmy dyed rabbit. Lined with cashmere, the label also says.

But they don't suit me. As Mother often said, I do not look *presentable* much of the time, presentable to her, I suppose, meaning fit to meet the Queen, and I never look *smart*. She is long dead, of course, having married my father (never very *presentable* or *smart* himself, come to think of it) when she was in her forties. I am fortunate not to have been a Downs child.

Still, I allowed myself a few moments of preening in front of the hall mirror. How nice to be the sort of woman who can wear a pair of gloves like this, perfectly matched to her puffy coat. Did I mention that she had auburn hair? I don't think it was dyed, though you can't tell these days, with all the tints available.

Such a beautiful woman.

I've wrapped the gloves in tissue paper. They're lying on my hall table. Waiting.

They were together in the deli this morning, Michael D and the woman. Michael D is fortyish, I would guess. The woman is younger, with blotchy skin. Michael D bought black coffee and a buttered roll and a *Times*. The woman made herself a cup of weak tea at the beverage stand, dunking a Lipton's bag a few times into hot water in the Styrofoam cup, then dropping it in the waste can. She stirred in two packets of sugar. I heard her say, "This should get me through." She took a sip, then made a small face and added, "I hope." Michael D picked up her briefcase and they walked together out to the car.

I forgot to add that she bought a magazine. One of those mass-market publications on having babies.

Mr. E has not been in for several days. His mother had a stroke, according to Mr. S. I have no reason to doubt him; Mr. E, a fussy balding bachelor in his fifties, seems like the sort of man who would live with his mother. But mindful of my own deception with Lancelot, I had to suppress a knowing smirk when Mr. S told me. His absence does come at an inconvenient time. I have had to take over the botany encyclopedia, putting aside the Etruscans.

I don't care for plants. I have only evergreens in front of my home, and they take care of themselves. On my first day at the company, Mr. E brought a bouquet of flowers, daisies I think they were, for my office, a tiny cubbyhole really but it's all mine. It was the first time anyone had ever given me flowers, and I guess I didn't know what to say. So I said nothing, let their appearance go unremarked. It never happened again.

There is a rumor going round that the foreign owners of our little operation are going to sell. I heard this on the elevator, discussed by the man and woman who run F_____ Publishing, my employer. I don't think they even know who I am; as I said earlier, I'm an invisible woman. But in a company so small, less than two dozen employees, surely they might be expected to recognize me. I do go to the company Christmas party every year, though I don't carry on and make a spectacle of myself like most of the others.

The man and the woman, Bill and Edith I call them in my mind's eye, the publisher and editor-in-chief respectively, said they didn't think it would come to much, the talk about selling.

She is pregnant, no doubt about it. Her coat was unbuttoned in the coffee shop this morning and I could tell from her tight-fitting clothes, the way expectant women dress these days, though goodness knows why, it's so unflattering, a cream silk shirt tucked into trim black wool slacks. A small pouch, under the waistline. Unmistakable. She had weak tea again.

Dora was so much prettier than this mouse-colored young woman. What does he see in her? Why give up a beautiful wife for a fling with—what? A co-worker? Someone he met at a bar?

And flaunting it, with his wife dead only a month.

She was buried upstate somewhere. Too far to take the gloves. They would look pretty on her grave, arranged like a pair of trysting bluebirds.

They remain on the hall table, wrapped in tissue.

Saturday I walked past their house for the first time since the accident. If it was an accident. The Toyota was in the driveway.

Isn't anyone bothered by this? Isn't anyone else concerned?

Tomorrow is the company Christmas party, though the holiday is still a few weeks away. The company holds it early, to save money, at B____'s, a small, no longer trendy restaurant several blocks away. After work, drinks and dinner. Bill and Edith were in the elevator again this morning. Nothing about the rumored sale. Though on the train in I read part of the *Journal* over someone's shoulder and learned that the German company, which has a long and unpronounceable and thoroughly ugly name, is divesting.

Perhaps I can mail them to him. Anonymously. Except that I'd have to take them in to the post office and have the package weighed and then it wouldn't really be anonymous.

He has to be made to *see*.

Mr. S for Stickler, which is what his name should be, had me in again this morning. Seems that I'm behind with the corrected galleys for H-L of the botany encyclopedia. That would be Hackberry through Lythraceae. I really don't know what he expects. I've told him that plants are foreign to me, and furthermore, the author's galleys are such a mess, owing to numerous entries being out of order (Hydrangea before Heliotrope, for example), with addenda in various colors of India ink (really: who uses fountain pens these days?), that I'm having a difficult time entering all the corrections. And at least a dozen pages of the manuscript have gone missing, presumably in Mr. E's office/cubbyhole.

Mr. E's mother has taken a turn for the worse. Perhaps she will die soon, and Mr. E will then return to work. After the funeral, of course.

I had hoped to do something with the gloves this weekend. Instead I'll have to spend time on the galleys, trying to make sense of all these corrections.

Well, I've finished, and turned them in. What an exhausting weekend I had. I did manage a brief walk up the hill and past the house on Sunday afternoon. Both the Volvo and the Toyota were in the driveway. And a For Sale sign is now on the front lawn.

I don't have much time. Houses go quickly in this town.

This morning Bill and Edith were on the elevator again. Really, it's quite annoying not to be recognized: I've spent so many years at this company. Neither of them said a thing. They seemed quite gloomy, as a matter of fact, preoccupied. Outsiders might think they'd had a lovers' quarrel, but I know better. Bill is gay, and Edith is married to a boy toy fifteen years her junior who always shows up at the Christmas party, as he did last week, wearing a loud tie and too much Polo cologne.

Wednesday. D-Day. The company is being sold. Bill made the announcement to all of us after we were summoned to the front reception area. He said he was very very very sorry to have to tell us this, one week before Christmas, and it was really a rotten, very rotten shame. Edith sucked in her cheeks and tried to look somber. Really, she has nothing to worry about. The boy toy is loaded; his father is something big in the pharmaceutical industry; I don't think he needs a job.

We are all losing our jobs, said Bill. Every last one of us. Because the Gebruder Spitzenhollern or whatever they're called is getting rid of all its U.S. holdings. It isn't as though they're about to fly us all to Berlin or Bonn or wherever else they have offices overseas. And I've forgotten my German.

Bill looked genuinely concerned. About himself, no doubt. I wonder if he has AIDS. I wonder if he'll get another job with the same insurance.

The books in their various stages, Etruscans, botany, Seychelles fruit flies and whatnot, will be sent overseas for completion. It seems that they all know English over there. How well, I ask myself, but of course that should not concern me.

Two days' notice. Two weeks' pay. Nothing else. But recommendations, of course, says Bill. We'll all get letters saying what good employees we've been. Why, every publisher in Manhattan would be lucky to have us. Blah, blah, blah.

Friday is my last day. You can bet I'm not going to do a single extra thing between now and then. I'm back on the Etruscans, but I'm washing my hands of Mr. E's encyclopedia. He's still out. His mother did not die. Does he really need this job? I have no idea.

What I do know is that *I* need this job. A job. Any job.

The tissue-wrapped gloves were the first thing I saw when I came home this evening. Still sitting on the hall table where I put them last week.

This can't wait. I'm doing it now.

But I didn't. It was dark, very dark, no moon, and soft snow was falling when I opened the door. I cannot make it up that hill at night, in snow.

The trains aren't running. We've had a blizzard, nearly nineteen inches in twelve hours. Wires are down. I called Mr. S and told him I couldn't make it in. I reminded him I still have sick time coming to me. This isn't a sick day, he said. You're well, aren't you? So I suppose I'll have a deduction from my last paycheck.

Friday. I made it in. No sign of Mr. E. I guess they'll mail him his check. Maybe someone will clean out his office and send his things, personal things, to him. Or maybe, like me, he has no possessions tucked away in desk drawers. There's a picture of an old woman who must be his mother on his desk, but I never saw anything else of a personal nature, unless you count the rather large paperweight, shaped like a human nose, flesh-toned. There's some lettering on the bridge, a name running vertically like a neon hotel sign. A brand of nose drops. I never commented on Mr. E's paperweight, thinking its provenance none of my business, and Mr. E never explained.

They made us wait till five o'clock, then passed out the checks. Lucky me, I was paid for yesterday. I guess the checks had already been made out before the storm by the Hassenpfefferspitzendrecker brothers, or whatever their names are. The checks are drawn on a Missouri bank, and they take a week to clear. Clever Krauts, ever playing the float.

At 5:02 p.m. I dropped Lancelot's picture into my tote bag, along with the form letter signed by Bill and Edith, and left the building. I did not say good-bye to Mr. S. A tactical error, perhaps, as he will no doubt be called by any future employer of mine. But I was most offended by his behavior. He actually came into my office before noon and demanded that I unpack my desk in his presence. He collected all my pencils (blue, red, green, number 2 black, most without any usable erasers), my nearly empty and quite gummy bottle of Wite-Out, my Scotch tape dispenser (how kind of him to let me keep the quarter roll of tape), my gummed flags in assorted colors, and my printer's rule. Printer's rules are expensive, so I can understand that, though mine was a giveaway from Galluzzi's Type in Brooklyn.

The streets were clear Saturday morning, the sun was shining.

I put the gloves in my tote bag, having removed Lancelot's picture and the form letter and my Scotch tape. I used a piece of the tape to fix the tissue paper securely. I put on my coat and my wool hat and my boots and a pair of mittens I use to shovel snow, and I headed up the hill. I had to walk in the street because some of my neighbors had not shoveled their walks. I cleaned mine on Thursday.

Michael D and Dora K's house is only a five-minute walk from my house, but it took fifteen, given the snow.

I noticed immediately that there were no cars in the driveway. But you never can tell.

The For Sale sign is still there. Because of the snow, probably.

I came up the walk and rang the bell.

I waited.

I rang the bell again.

No answer.

I tried to look through the front windows, standing on tiptoes and craning my head. Discreetly, of course. I didn't want neighbors to call the police.

I could not see a thing in the living room to the right, or what must have been the dining room on the left. Not a stick of furniture, not a scrap of carpet. Priscilla curtains at the front windows, but people often leave curtains behind when they move.

Which is what Michael D has done, it seems. Sometime in the last seven days he moved away.

Was the blotchy-faced woman with him?

Will they marry now, having escaped from the House of Death, as one of the tabs called it with trashy exaggeration? Though perhaps that was a good name for it, a Tudor, rather gloomy if the truth be known. A marriage had died there: wasn't that evident? She was crying on the train the day before she was killed.

And he killed her. I do not doubt it. Not by pushing her in front of the train but by breaking her heart. She was already dead the last day I saw her.

There was nothing to do but walk back to my own house down the hill. I could not leave the gloves behind: he was gone, and strangers would not want them.

Nor can I throw them away. They are human, somehow, deserving of life. I put them on my hall closet shelf, next to a tweed hat, a pipe, a silver flute in a black leather case, a dozen or so coins, handkerchiefs, a Tiffany key ring and other objects left behind by the dead. All wrapped in tissue. All waiting for their owners to reclaim them. The hat tumbled off the head of a middle-aged man who collapsed on the street near the office a few years ago. Another man, elderly, dropped the pipe while walking his chihuahua in Central Park. Oddly, he held on firmly to the leash as he went down; a result of the involuntary seizure, I suppose. I am glad of that, his clasping; I would not have known what to do with a dog. Mementoes of the dead, bits and pieces of lives suddenly ended, innocent people struck, stricken while going about their business. But there were a few suicides, too. A few *others*, I should say. Including the young woman, a girl really, who jumped from the A train platform and left behind her flute. It wasn't worth much: I had it appraised a few months later. It isn't as though I was *stealing* valuable property.

What I do, have done, is noble: Commemorations of the Dead is what I call my collection. In my closet they live on through personal objects. I take them down from time to time, touch them, stroke them. I remember all the names.

The blue gloves were the only part of my collection I have ever tried to return. But I think you understand the impulse, and I hope you are sympathetic. *Attention must be paid*, to quote the immortal Mrs. Loman. The blue-gloved woman died of a broken heart, and though my Presbyterian mother might have begged to disagree, it was my task, not that of an impersonal, cruel, and distant god, to seek vengeance. Just seeing him open the tissue, and then the flicker of fear that told me he knew that *I* knew: I was only after that. It would have been enough.

I could still follow him. It's not too late. Track him down. (We are good at research, obnoxiously good, those of us who correct other people's mistakes for a living.) March up to his new door and thrust the package in his face and say *Didn't you forget something?*

But I have put them away, up on the shelf, tucked behind the flute and the pipe and the Tiffany ring with the single key to a nameless door.

Whoever finds me, what will they—*he* or *she*—make of my collection? Perhaps they will say *She was a woman of mystery*, and the neighbors, when asked, will concur

I have decided not to leave a note. Let them find me. Let them make of me what they will.

Shelter

Mama wasn't too bad today. I mean she didn't start complaining the minute I walked in, about the sheets not being smooth enough, or how Tywanda, the nurse's aide, hadn't warmed the bedpan, which they bring in before visiting hours to avoid accidents. She was even sitting up in one of the chairs by the bed, and she had a stack of magazines on her lap. The chairs are upholstered in marbleized green plastic with chrome arms and legs, like those kitchen dinette sets from the Fifties. I have a set of my own, Mama's and Daddy's. Mine's original and I bet these chairs are too, and worth a fortune. I saw one on *Antiques Road Show* just last week. Despite the fact that they're not that comfortable. Which is the point, of course: nursing homes don't want visitors staying too long. Upsets their routine.

I come to see Mama every weekend, mostly on Sundays. As I said, she usually lays into me right away. "But it's not you," the nurse, that's Anabelle, the head nurse, not Tywanda, tells me, by way I guess of trying to be kind. Or hoping for a nice Christmas present since it's getting to be that time of year. She'll take me aside and she'll tell me Mama's like that most of the time. There's no pleasing her, no matter how hard they try. They make an effort, I know, but let's face it, Mama's a difficult woman. Daddy used to say that about her, though of course not within her hearing.

But today, glory of glories, she had magazines, and guess what they were: *Photoplay*s. Seems that old Mrs. Simmons down the hall passed on last week, and she left behind a bunch of *Coronet*s and *Look*s and *Modern Screen*s and such, which haven't been around for years. And Tywanda, because she knows Mama loves the movies, about the only thing you could say Mama does love, Tywanda pulled the movie magazines out of the pile and gave them to Mama. At least that's what Anabelle says, though she may be trying to put Tywanda in a good light. Christmas again. Tywanda seems pretty smart to me. She could get a job almost anyplace I bet, even that high-toned Mirror Arms in Brentwood. I bet Anabelle's scared to death half the time she's going to lose her.

Anyway, Mama had half a dozen *Photoplay*s on her lap and she was goo-gooing and cackling and *ooh*ing and *aah*ing. Used to read them myself when I was a kid. Over forty years ago, and we'll leave it at that. I don't reveal my age. When did they stop? Putting them out, I mean? TV took over, I guess, and that's what killed the movie magazines. I didn't notice, back then. I was busy with other things, like marrying a man who turned out wrong. Can't say that Mama didn't warn me, but after a while with Mama you kind of turned a deaf ear because she said the same negative thing about everything and everybody.

Except little Susan Villette.

My oh my, how she loved that child. Saw all her movies. Dragged me to them and made me sit through hours and hours of this cutesy little blonde thing, eight years old when she made her first picture but she was small and they palmed her off as four. The stories were always the same. Little Susan—playing Paula, Cathie, Nicole, Jenny, Cindy, Margaret, Alice, whathaveyou—was an orphan or a kid sister or adopted. She wasn't the star—that was usually some big-timer like Ray Milland or Robert Young or Dana Andrews paired with Jane or June or Lana or, in a pinch, simpering Donna Reed—but she still had a big role. Susan Villette wasn't her real name either. I think it was Polish or Czech or from someplace else over there, what we used to call the Iron Curtain nations. Not that Susan spoke with an accent; she was born here. I know this for a fact because once, when Louella Parsons was interviewing her on the radio, she said that Susan was so smart she just might grow up to be the first woman President, and as we all know, you have to be born in the USA for that to happen.

Mama loved little Susan's hair, fixed in ringlets with a big bow. I was, and still am, thanks to Antoinette at the Clip 'n' Dip, a brunette, and my hair back then was stick straight, but Mama wrapped it in papers every Saturday night so I'd have curls for Sunday School the next morning. The results never pleased her: try as she might, my hair never waved. Once she even gave me a Tonette home permanent, saying the whole time she was putting on the smelly lotion that it was a waste of time and good money, and sure enough it was. So were the bows she mounted on my head with scratchy bobbie pins. They looked like dead butterflies. "If only," Mama would sigh, giving my Sunday taffeta a last tug over my plump stomach and reminding me to hold my shoulders back. I knew what she meant: if only I looked like Susan Villette.

Or sounded like her. She was on the radio a lot, being interviewed by Louella or Louella's big rival, Hedda Hopper, shows Mama adored. When Louella chirped "And now for my first exclusive!" I thought Mama was having a stroke, she shook so much. Susan had a sweet, dear little voice, like one of God's own angels, said Mama. Daddy privately expressed the opinion that she talked like a bottle of vanilla, which from the way he said it didn't sound so good. Ah, Mama sighed. If only.

But I didn't, and couldn't, and never even tried, which Mama attributed to willful behavior inherited from Daddy's side of the family. So you can imagine how glad I was when Susan Villette stopped making pictures. Daddy, who tried to offer what he thought was reassurance when Mama wasn't around, told me she'd no doubt grown big and gawky, now she'd become a teenager. She was a few years older than me, so I must have been about twelve then. I was definitely big and gawky already.

After a while Mama stopped talking about Susan Villette. Poor little Susan just faded away, gone and forgotten. I don't recall thinking about her even once in years. And then one day last week, out of the blue, I met her, big as life.

And I do mean big. There she was, standing in front of me in the checkout line at the Vons on Pico. Only I didn't know it at first. I just knew I'd been standing there for what seemed forever, holding a can of LeSueur peas and a shrink-wrapped pork chop and one of those pineapples they fly in from Hawaii and tell you it's fresh-picked and charge extra. I don't waste money, but I like to eat well. Anyway, I'm standing in line while the cashier, a kid wearing multiple studs in both ears, is having an argument with some old lady two ahead of me because she claims the Sunsweet Prunes are on special and he says no they're not and she says then call the manager. Well, after what seems like an eternity *that* gets settled (she buys only one box of the prunes; they aren't on special; I have to give the kid credit), and then I'm only one person away from checking out so I can get home in time for *Unsolved Mysteries*, reruns but that's okay. The fat lady in front of me wrapped in a ratty mink because the Santa Ana winds are blowing writes a check for two potatoes, an onion, a package of hamburger, and a pack of cigarettes, Luckies. I didn't know anybody smoked them anymore. And fifty dollars over, she says. The kid asks for ID, which she produces, and then holds the check up to the register, beside a list of names. Sorry, the kid says, turning back to face her. We can't take any checks from—and he reads the name out loud—"*Susan Villette*." Well, you could have knocked me over with a feather.

While she stands there hemming and hawing and pretending to look through her purse for cash I take a long look at her. I can't believe this is what has become of little Susan Villette. Well, for one thing she's now Big Susan. Whereas I trimmed down in my teens and have remained slim ever since, Susan Villette is, well, obese, with the kind of puffy face Mama says comes from drink, and badly dyed reddish-blond hair so thin you can see her scalp, and her hands are brown-spotted, with untrimmed nails. Now I have my share of faults just like anybody else, and I can't say I'm above taking secret pleasure in the fall of the mighty from grace, something I've tried to work on for years with the help of my minister, Mr. Cove. But today, whatever Mr. Cove's been preaching for years and years, about being kind to one's neighbor and all that, must have sunk in, because before I know it I'm offering to pay for Susan Villette's potatoes, onion, and hamburger. Not the cigarettes, but the kid's already rung them up. What I say, in the sweetest voice I can manage, is "Miss Villette, I'll take care of this for you—you can pay me back sometime."

"My my my," says Susan Villette, still sifting through her purse. Her voice is scratchy, from the Luckies no doubt. "I thought I had a twenty in here but I guess it must be in my other pocketbook."

Yeah, sure. "Allow *me*," I say, and offer the kid a ten and a five.

"You are just *too* kind," Susan Villette rasps, snapping her purse shut. She grabs the plastic bag and fourteen cents in change and heads toward the door. She can't walk very fast; as I said, she's a big woman.

"Wait just a minute!" I go after her, leaving pork chop, peas, and pineapple on the conveyor belt. "You don't know my name, or where I live."

"Should I?" she says. A bit airily, I think. We are blocking the door. Two old men pushing a single cart make a fuss as they maneuver round us.

"I just bought your groceries."

"You needn't be so testy. I intend to repay you."

"Hey, lady! I gotta line here. You gonna buy these or what?"

"Save them—I'll come back later." Susan Villette is already waddling, and that's the word for it, out the door. But it's easy to follow her.

She lives in a walkup a few blocks east on Pico, above a used bookstore next to the post office. I like the post office: lots of people from the islands working there, and they have such a good time, whooping and hollering and making their sassy jokes, you almost don't mind when the line starts stretching out the door. It's entertainment, pure and simple. The clerk I like best has bananas painted on her nails, with a splash of glitter. Or maybe they're crescent moons. I don't want to stare.

But the point is, I had seen Susan Villette before. A lot. In the post office. And didn't have a clue who she was. You see, I get my mail at a post box. An old habit. I started years ago, when Mama came to live with me and went snooping through every piece I got. Not that I get anything I want to hide, let me make that perfectly clear. Some people send away for things, you know, racy private things, but not me. I have no interest in that sort of stuff. Never have. Now my husband, former husband, did, but that's another story. Anyway, I just wanted to protect my privacy because Mama would get the mail every day before I got home from the real estate office where I work over on Beverly Glen, which is only about a mile from our house, and she'd open it, even the junk mail, and she'd write things on it, such as, "I wouldn't let these people send letters to me, if I were you." And I'd say, "Mama, it's just an advertisement for some cruise"—or a vacuum cleaner, or free coffee, or, once, a whole set of china painted with Ronald Reagan's face—"and you need not worry yourself about it because I have no intention of replying." And finally I just got tired of the whole thing. That was the day I came home and she'd *washed* the mail. Yes, washed it, in a sinkful of Joy, then pinned it all to the clothesline out back. It was dirty, she said; looked like the mailman had dropped it in mud.

I've had the postbox five years now, three with Mama, two since Mama's move to Altaview, and it's worked out just fine. I pick up the mail on my way home from work. I'm walking, you understand. Everybody's astonished at that, by the way. "What, you don't have a car? This is L.A. You *have* to drive." And I'm here to say you don't. I walk a lot, that's how I keep my figure. In a pinch there's a bus for Santa Monica and the beach. If you ask me, Susan Villette would be a lot better off if she walked around more—but I'm getting ahead of myself. So anyway, I'm at the post office every afternoon, mornings on Saturday, and three days out of six I swear I see Susan Villette, the woman I've learned is Susan Villette, in the post office. She's noticeable, you might even say *arresting,* because there aren't a lot of fat people in Los Angeles. At least on the streets. Everybody's kind of image-conscious here. As a rule, fat people stay home.

So what was Susan Villette doing in the post office so much? Not getting her mail. Knowing what I know now, she couldn't afford a post box anyway. No. Susan Villette, former screen star, was working there as a janitor. Every time I saw her in the post office, she was dragging a big green plastic garbage bag. Susan Villette collected the post office trash.

I was putting two and two together when I followed Susan Villette out of Vons and up Pico. I knew where she lived because I'd asked Banana Nails about her; I wondered if she was a homeless person camping out at the post office. "Oh, she be a real nice lady. Need a job so Smokey"—that's our local postmaster—"he hire her. He feel real sorry for peoples like that, see her at Jack 'n the Box eatin' fries, ask if she like a job. She say yes." Banana Nails has an engaging smile, lots of flashing goldwork in her teeth. I think she's Jamaican, like Tywanda. "Real convenient 'cause she live next door, right upstairs from MisterBooks."

I caught up with Susan Villette at the light. "You dropped this," I said, handing her the sales receipt.

She'd slipped on a pair of dark glasses with pointy red plastic frames, Jato glasses we used to call them way back when; vintage. She could sell them on e-Bay.

The light changed. We crossed Overland together.

"I know who you are," I said, in what I hoped was a friendly tone. "I saw all your movies when I was young."

"I'm not old," she snapped.

"Of course not," I said. "I didn't say you were."

We passed MisterBooks. I paused but she kept on walking. Though she'd slowed down. It was too hot in the sunshine for a mink coat, and, as I said, she's fat. "This is your home, isn't it?" I called after her, stopping at a doorway between the bookstore and a Thai restaurant. A low-end eatery, smelling of rotten cilantro. I know it well; I used to bring home takeout for Mama.

"Come on back. You can give me the money later." And because I guess I look harmless, or maybe she was tired, she stopped and turned around.

"I was really and truly a fan," I say. Mr. Cove would call that a lie. Mama was the fan. Truth to tell, I hated and resented little Susan Villette. But big Susan, grown-up Susan is another matter. The jury, as they say, is still out, plus there's the matter of fifteen dollars. She has a job, she could pay me back. She could sell the glasses and buy a cheaper pair. I live on a fixed income. I will be old myself someday and no one will hire me. And there's Mama's upkeep to think about, though Daddy's GI benefits take care of most of it.

We're standing at the door, her door. "So name the movies," she says, looking me over. The cilantro smell is nauseating.

I recite the titles, not all but enough.

"And your favorite?"

A test, no doubt. "*Springtime for Sally*," I blurt out without thinking.

"Mine, too," she says, and leads the way upstairs.

The place isn't as bad as you might imagine. A single bed with brown chenille spread, dresser topped with a crocheted scarf and one of those frilly-shaded hobnail milk glass lamps. Slipcovered sofa and matching chair in a dull brown, frayed but intact. Dining alcove with card table, folding chair, a hotplate in the corner. Mismatched plates and cups and glasses on a metal TV tray. The TV's an old console hunched in the corner, with rabbit ears on top.

"Refrigerator's in here," she says, and ducks through a bead curtain to empty the plastic bag.

It's clean, sort of; there's no loose trash lying around. Nothing personal either, no photographs, books, magazines in sight. It might be a room in a cheap hotel, one of those SROs downtown. Not that I've ever been in one, but you hear stories.

"So it's not the Ambassador," she says, re-emerging through the curtain. She shrugs off the mink and lights a cigarette. "I had my own suite there, once. 'Little Susan Villette' written on the door in glitter, fancy that, and a tiny star for a peephole." She's wearing what used to be called a housedress, a cotton print with buttons down the front. I didn't know they made them anymore.

She opens a dresser drawer and pulls out a bottle. "Like a drink?"

Muscatel. Mama's remedy for female problems. I shake my head.

She pours half a glassful, drops the bottle back in the drawer, and plops down on the sagging sofa. "Can't give you back your money right now, so there's no point in asking." She kicks off a pair of pumps, stained blue satin. "Belonged to June Allyson," she says. "Wore 'em in my last picture." The shoes have cut deep ovals in her fleshy feet.

I sit on the edge of the club chair. I'm not ready to leave yet.

"You must have more like that," I said, meaning the shoes. "Other souvenirs?"

"Like I told you, I don't have any money," she says irritably, taking a drag on the Lucky, ignoring the question. She's drained the glass in a gulp.

There's a closet over by the bed, which is high off the ground; plenty of room underneath. The chenille spread hides all.

"Look, you got your kicks, if that's what you want. Yeah, I recognize you now. The lady who's always in the post office. So what's your game?"

And that's when I came up with my plan.

Well, of course I didn't tell Mama all this when I saw her today. Mama, truth to tell, is losing her mind, though they don't say that nowadays. They have fancy words for all those things that happen to old people, but they all amount to the same thing. Which is living somewhere else, the past or another country or maybe the future tucked inside their heads. Oh, Mama still recognizes me but you can tell she's wandering down another road. Anabelle and Tywanda both have noticed it. Anabelle says she's getting dementia, though not necessarily Alzheimer's; it seems there's lots of different kinds. Tywanda puts it a little differently: "Honey, she don't know where she's at sometimes, but just between you and me that's just fine. Hope when I gotta be shut up in a place like this *I* got somewhere else in my mind to go to."

Mama's place, of course, is the movies, old movies. They have the TCM channel at Altaview, and Mama can watch it most anytime she wants. For Christmas last year I got her an autographed photo of Robert Osborne. Mama loves those interviews he does with old-time stars; she just thinks they're the best. I came in to visit one Sunday when they were showing his chat with Betty Hutton, and Mama was sitting there with tears streaming down her face as Betty described her hard life and how she found God and He made it all better. Mama wouldn't let me speak till the show was over, and by that time visiting hours were almost over too. Which was okay; visiting Mama, as I said before, can be a trial. Things go better when she has something else to do while I'm there. Like today, with the stack of *Photoplay*s.

I didn't say boo when she found one with Susan Villette on the cover. "Oh, will you look at that!" said Mama. "You remember that pretty little thing?" She touched the picture gently with a forefinger topped by a laminated red nail. I pay extra for Mama's weekly manicures.

"Why of course I do," I cooed back. Indeed I do.

"You'd think that Mr. Osborne would have her on sometime," said Mama. "I wonder why not?" She was thumbing through the magazine, looking for the cover story.

"Mmmm," I said. "I have no idea." I wonder if I have to tell this to Mr. Cove.

"You think we could write Mr. Osborne about it?"

"Mmmm." But Mama had found the Susan Villette story and started to read it aloud, and it was time to leave.

"I don't have a 'game,'" I told Susan Villette. "I just tried to help you out is all, back there at Vons."

"Nobody helps Susan," she said, flicking ashes on the carpet. "Nobody gives a damn. Agent took just about all I earned, Mom and Dada stole the rest." She gave me a real angry look, like she could kill me, but I knew it wasn't me personally she was mad at. Though I guess the fact that I dress well and have my figure and don't have to push a broom at the post office didn't exactly make her happy either.

"What if somebody did care, one of your old fans, say, what if they really truly wanted to help—what would you ask them to do for you?" I was trying to draw her out a little, before I mentioned my plan.

Well, you're not going to believe this, or maybe you will, depending on your circumstances, but when I said those words, big old Susan Villette blubbered like a baby.

"I just want a real home so bad," she said between sobs. "Look at this dump—why should I have to live in a place like this?"

"Why, you most certainly should not," I said, leaning toward her and offering my clean handkerchief.

She daubed her eyes and blew her nose noisily. "It's just so unfair is all," she said, sniffling.

"Of course it is," I replied. "And that's why I'm offering to take you home. You can live with *me*."

Getting Susan Villette and her things over to Veteran wasn't too bad, though she had far more stuff than I'd imagined. The closet by the bed, as I suspected, was stacked with sagging cardboard boxes; Susan said they were filled with photo albums, yellowed clippings, more shoes worn by costars. Plus another closet in the bathroom, more of the same. And three footlockers under the bed crammed with movie outfits, dainty taffeta dresses with lace collars and ribbon sashes, tiny matching skirts and jackets in velvet-trimmed moth-holed wool, in colors you don't see anymore, maroon and such. And costumes, cutesy little spangled numbers from once upon a time, rolled up in crumbly tissue, leaking sequins. Did I tell you she danced, too? Mama made me take tap and ballet for *five* years on account of that. There was less, much less, other stuff, housedresses, raggedy underwear, two pairs of old-lady tie shoes, Enna Jetticks they were called. Mama refuses to wear them. Anyway, it took four trips in the taxi to move it all.

I got ahead of myself just a bit. I have to tell you she was absolutely *thrilled*, there's no other word for it, when I made my suggestion. No haughty, hoity-toitiness after that, nosiree. She practically fell all over me, hugging, kissing my face, hands. I think she might have even tried to kiss my feet but she was too fat to bend down.

We moved her over, I did, with the taxi, that very day. I'd left work early, it was slow, and Bernice, that's my boss, told me I could just scoot right out of there. Which is why I happened to be in Vons at three-thirty on a Friday afternoon. Anyway, to continue, I moved Susan Villette straight into Mama's old room. I'd cleaned it out a few years ago, given away to Goodwill most of Mama's bric-a-brac. Mama liked to collect those little figurines they sold at Woolworth's, the ones they made in Occupied Japan once upon a time, dogs with silly grins, little boys in sailor suits, full-skirted ladies. She took a few to Altaview. Maybe I should have kept more. But the bed, Mama's iron bed, was there, and her double dresser with the crocheted scarf she made in high school, and the framed picture of that farm couple praying out in the potato field, the one you see everywhere, or used to. Mama got her own bed years ago, when Daddy passed on. The closet was big enough for Susan's clothes. We left her boxes in the front room. That would be her project, she said. Going through all that stuff, sorting it out. Maybe she could sell a few things, she said. Maybe so, I replied.

Things have gone smoothly so far. Susan pretty much keeps to herself. I had to say a few words about keeping the bathroom tidy; she brought an old hatbox full of cosmetics, leaking bottles of perfumes and lotions, smeary lipsticks and such, and she likes to use them all. I didn't tell you, did I, that she wears *lots* of makeup. Though it doesn't do much to hide what Mama used to call wear-and-tear. Most of the stuff is old, and I mean *really* old. Like, for example, she has some Pansticks that might be originals, used by Max Factor himself. And the rouge and lipsticks have this rancid rotten smell. Plus she has brands of perfume that aren't even made anymore, like Tweed. Not a name that goes with a former child actress; maybe it belonged to Jane or June or one of her other costars. I looked through the cosmetic stuff Friday night, after she went to bed. She'd left it scattered all over.

Well, we got through the first night okay. For supper I'd picked up takeout at Jack in the Box and put my pork chop in the freezer. Jack in the Box isn't really my kind of place, but Susan likes it. On Saturday I didn't want to leave her alone, not that soon anyway, so I stayed home, finding little things for myself to do like dusting my collection of Dolls from Other Lands, which Daddy bought me when I was a little girl. They're still sitting in the front room, in the glass case he built himself. I have sixteen, not the whole set though Daddy did his best. On a bus driver's salary I'd say that's pretty darn good. Susan stayed in bed most of the day. I looked in on her a few times, just to make sure she was still alive. I guess it's a big relief for her, having a place to stay and not having to worry about paying rent. She's a trusting soul, or maybe she's too old and too worn out to give much thought to what might happen next.

Saturday night I fixed enchiladas with Susan's onion and hamburger from Vons. She came out of her room, Mama's room, lured I guess by the smells. It's a small house, one of those little stucco ranches with an orange tile roof. Daddy bought it when I was six years old, with a GI loan. Anyway, she comes waddling down the hall and sets herself down at the kitchen table, which I mentioned before, I do believe. It's original Formica, plus four matching chairs padded with red plastic. I'm holding on to it because someday in the not too distant future it will fetch a high price on e-Bay. I'm sure of it. Well, Susan ate most of the enchiladas and then she went back to bed. I should add that she made a pretty little speech about how grateful she was and all. I guess they taught her manners, those studio folks, all those years ago.

I decided to skip church on Sunday, since I had a houseguest. I think Mr. Cove will understand. I fixed a big breakfast, pancakes, sausage, fresh-squeezed juice, and Susan came out to eat of her own accord. The woman has an appetite, I can say that for sure. Then I had to get ready to go to the Altaview. What was I supposed to do with Susan? Didn't want to take her with me. Not yet anyway. "You have something you fancy doing today?" I asked. "Because I have to visit a friend this afternoon—but of course I don't want to leave you . . . " I hadn't mentioned Mama to her yet; best keep her in the dark.

"Oh, I've got plenty to do," says Susan. "There's all these boxes."

Well, with some anxiety I left her there, sitting in the front room, *ooh*ing and *aah*ing in her housecoat and slippers. I was only gone two hours, counting the bus ride; Mama, as I said before, had the *Photoplay*s for company. When I got back Susan Villette was still there, on the floor. I had to help her back on her feet so she could go outside and have a smoke. I've told her smoking inside is not allowed, that's my only rule.

Sundays I like to get Chinese after I see Mama; once a week doesn't hurt though you have to worry about salt and that other stuff. I usually eat out, at a little place over on Pico, but Susan didn't seem to want to walk anywhere so I went over and brought it back myself. Susan, I realize, is costing me money. The taxis weren't cheap, plus there's my fifteen dollars (minus the hamburger and onion) and all the food she's eating. So far she hasn't offered to pay. But I'm biding my time.

Tonight, after the egg foo yung and spring rolls, I brought up the post office. Are you planning to go back to work, I asked in a neutral-sounding voice. Oh, I don't know about that, says Susan. (She's got Social Security, she says, but not much. Which seems kind of odd on account of how much money she must have made years ago, but Susan says her mama and daddy got paid, not little Susan, so she didn't get the credits.) But you need something to *do*, *will* need something to do, after you get your things sorted out, I said. And could have added but didn't that she hasn't made much progress in that direction. Today when I came home she had one of the albums in her lap, opened to a page of old black-and-white snapshots, the kind you used to take with a Brownie camera. I didn't see anything set aside. Truth to tell, a lot of her stuff may be junk, but after she goes to bed I'm going to have a look for myself. She's been working at the post office on Tuesdays and Fridays. I have a day to get her back on the job.

Monday morning I have to be at work at nine sharp. A lot of homes are sold on the weekend, and Bernice has a ton of paper to process. That's what I do, get the contracts ready for the lawyers, plus there's online work too, taking homes off the multilist, putting new homes on, etc. etc. *Homes.* We never say *houses* in this business. Not allowed to. I've been working in real estate close to thirty years; I know the rules.

Before that I had a job at Bullock's, in the lingerie department. They gave nice discounts; I still have two silk nightgowns I bought there and I wish I'd held on to the fox stole and didn't give it up when people stopped wearing draped furs. Everything comes back into style one way or another. I quit Bullock's when I got married. Mr. H we'll call him (that's H for husband; I don't want to be any more specific than that) didn't want me to work. Which was fine with me. Thought we'd move out to Ventura, have a family, but it didn't happen. Spent three years in a rental duplex in Culver City doing the happy housewife bit except I stopped being happy. Mr. H was a salesman; ladies underwear, wholesale. That's how I met him in the first place, though I think he was aiming too high with Bullock's. Anyway, it wasn't really a marriage. And I found out he had what I'll call peculiar interests related to underwear. I didn't tell Mama and Daddy about the divorce for almost a year. And then I moved back home. By that time I'd gotten my job with the realty company. Bernice is my third and best boss there. I've got nothing to complain about.

What I started to say is that Sunday night I usually go to bed early because Bernice expects me promptly the next morning. But this Sunday was going to be different. So far, except for the hatbox and trunks, I hadn't really looked through Susan's things. But I couldn't put it off much longer. So I made sure Susan had a good belt of muscatel after supper and she was back on Mama's iron bed snoring by nine. I stayed up till one a.m. or thereabouts.

I had too much work Monday morning to take my usual coffee break, so I couldn't make the call till afternoon. I took a late lunch at my desk, one to two, another girl in the office brought me carryout from Hamburger Hamlet, and after I'd finished eating, the conference room was empty so I went in there to use the phone. I needed privacy, which is something you don't get in a cubicle. It wasn't that hard to find Mr. Osborne. I was surprised, since he's a big star in his own right. Of course I had to talk to three different people first but then his voice came on the line. I have to tell you I was excited. Living out here you tend to get blasé if that's the word about film stars and such, and I'm not the movie fan Mama was and is, but still, I do watch TCM from time to time. Some nights when there's nothing much else to do after I've cleaned up from supper and rinsed out my pantyhose and programmed the Mr. Coffee, I look in the cable guide and find a Joan or Bette black-and-white something.

I've seen them all, of course, some with Mama and/or Daddy in the theater way back when, though I don't care to admit my age.

"You have something to tell me about Susan Villette?" says Mr. Osborne in that wonderful voice he has. He could have been a movie star himself I bet.

"Yes indeed I do," I say, trying to make my voice stop shaking, I'm that excited. I've told myself I'm going to wait to ask about the interview, because of Susan's present appearance of course; that's something that's going to have to go, as they say, on the back burner. So I launch into telling him how I found her, I try to be brief, not going into too many details about Vons though I do point out that I bought her groceries which is how she came to be living in my house, I mean home, at this very moment. But more than that, I continue, before he can comment on this piece of information, more important is that she has these absolutely fantastic movie collectibles, pictures, autographs, clothing, even one of Judy-Dorothy's ruby slippers of all things. It must be worth a fortune, I say, and since he knows so much about the film business can he tell me where I might want to try selling all this? Before putting it on e-Bay, maybe to some museum? And because I will try to do all I can for Mama till her dying day I don't forget to add: Susan isn't in very good shape right now, of course, the way she's been living has taken its toll, shall we say, but Mr. Osborne's welcome to do an interview whenever he wishes, whenever Susan's ready to go before the camera again.

Well, I say all this pretty quickly, blurting it out as fast as I can because the conference room is booked for two p.m. and it's now one fifty-seven. Someone, Bernice, is coming in to get it ready. By the way I do not tell Mr. Osborne, though I am telling you now and want to make it perfectly clear: I fully intend, *intended* to split any proceeds with my church.

I think maybe the phone has gone dead because there's no reply from Mr. Osborne. "Hello?" I ask. "Hello? Hello?"

Bernice is laying out yellow pads and pencils around the table and reaches my elbow when his voice finally comes back on. "Susan Villette can't be at your house," says Mr. Osborne quietly. "I just saw her yesterday. Did an interview with her in Sherman Oaks. She's been living there for twenty years."

But Mr. Osborne is very interested in the boxes, the trunks and what's inside them, the pictures, albums, clothes, especially the ruby slipper. Bernice is beside me, looking at her watch. "I'll call you back," I say hurriedly and hang up.

"Not long distance, I hope," says Bernice.

"Of course not," I say. "Local. Having to do with Mama." Which is not quite a lie.

Well, they've traced the call, those folks at TCM. Two detectives showed up at the office around four o'clock. I heard them talking to Bernice, who's on the other side of my cubicle. Some lady made a call from here to Robert Osborne a few hours ago, they said. Any idea who it was?

Bernice says no she does not and adds that she is very very busy and she's sorry she can't help them. Well, one of the men says, it's a matter of stolen property, lady, and we have reason to believe somebody in your office has that stolen property. "Doris?" Bernice calls over the wall. "Maybe you can help these gentlemen—?"

There's no point in putting it off, I've been shaking in my shoes for the past two hours, so I lead them down to the conference room and tell them as calmly as I can the whole story of how I met Susan Villette and brought her home. I make a point of saying several times how I bought her groceries, and my plans to share anything from selling her stuff.

"Make that past tense, sister," says the shorter detective, who looks a little like Jack Webb but less Italian. "You aren't selling anything. That property you got doesn't belong to you *or* your houseguest."

"Yeah, that's right," says the other detective. He has acne-pocked skin. "And that old lady you got living at your house, she's not Susan Villette."

Well, that's hardly news. I didn't see how Mr. Osborne had any reason to lie. The taller guy, Scarface, doesn't seem very bright to me. Shorty, on the other hand, gets to the point. "Susan Villette's maid stole a bunch of personal property, five, six years ago. Then she disappeared. Looks like it's wound up at your house. Along with the maid."

I can't leave till five, I tell them. I still have contracts to mail out.

"We'll wait," says Shorty.

When I was little, Mama used to tell me I trusted people too much. Back in the first grade, say, when I'd let myself get talked into swapping lunch with the other kids and wind up with baloney and mustard on day-old white, plus a brown banana for dessert. Or later, loaning my periwinkle blue cashmere twinset, my *only* cashmere twinset, to my best friend, Eileen, who gave it back spattered with India ink. Life's full of tricks is what Mama told me, time and time again. Daddy had no opinion on the subject, just kept his own counsel, as they say. Even when I had to tell him about Mr. H, Daddy never saw any use in pointing out the obvious.

Well, all the movie stuff is gone. And, for the time being, so is Miriam Hassenmosek aka Susan Villette. Shorty was right: Miriam was Susan's longtime maid, an Iron Curtain refugee back in the Sixties. After thirty years, Susan had to let her go. The usual story, drinking too much, stealing little things here and there, crystal ashtrays, pickle forks and the like. So when Susan's out, Miriam packs up the movie stuff, a lot but not all of it, plus she takes some ID, and settles herself in a walkup in West LA. Susan doesn't discover what's missing till months later, when she goes looking for that ruby slipper. Planned to donate it to a charity auction at the children's hospital, Shorty told me.

Miriam's in jail, but Susan Villette doesn't want to press charges. So after the court hearing, Miriam's going to be released on probation. Into my custody.

I don't mind the company, and Mr. Cove says the church will help with expenses if need be.

Mr. Osborne's interview with Susan Villette, the real Susan Villette, was on last night, primetime, eight to nine. I made a special point of watching it with Mama, though Wednesday's not my usual visiting day. Anabelle let me stay past visiting hours, which end at 8:30. Mama's going downhill pretty fast now; I don't think she really knew who she was looking at up there on the screen when Susan Villette was talking to Mr. Osborne. But Mama did come alive for the film clips of young Susan, pretty, smiling, charming, singing, dancing young Susan Villette. And I have to say that old Susan looks pretty darn good too. She's aged well, as they say. Like Jane Powell. And much, much better than Deanna Durbin, who won't show her face in public anymore, or so I understand.

Miriam stayed home last evening. AMC had a good Western on with Randolph Scott, one of her favorites she says. She's looking better. I've had her in to the Clip 'n' Dip a few times, and my Vietnamese manicurist over on Pico does wonders with her nails. Miriam's started taking short walks in the neighborhood, and the pounds are coming off. Weaning her off the muscatel is taking longer, but I'm making progress. Ditto the smoking. Saturday we're going to the beach. If it doesn't rain.

Meanwhile, I notice she's taken a real interest in my Dolls from Other Lands, sitting in Daddy's glass case in the front room. The little Czech girl especially. It reminds her of home, Miriam told me. I think I'm going to let her keep it on Mama's dresser, Miriam's dresser now. I don't think Daddy would mind.

Waving at Trains

One day in late December, I must have been seven, Daddy brought home a railroad calendar to hang on the kitchen wall. A new year was coming. We lived in the country then. The house was small, with cinders in the backyard instead of grass, and beyond the cinders an asbestos-shingled coop for Rhode Island reds that gave us eggs. The calendar was a simple affair, a broad piece of stiff cardboard with a metal-rimmed hole at the top for hanging, and a gummed packet of sheets, one for each month, stapled at the bottom. You ripped one off as each month passed. There was only one picture, at the top, and it was supposed to last the year. But I didn't mind. It showed a house on a flat piece of land, with a railroad track running alongside and a cornfield in the distance. The picture was a painting, the Lichtenstein comic-book kind, in Crayola colors (the basic box of eight: Red and Blue and Yellow and Black and Green, no Flesh or Siena). In the picture a train traveled along the track, right to left, and a little girl with black braids leaned out the window of the house, smiling and waving. Inside the train faces smiled, hands waved back. That little girl, that's me, I thought: how nice to watch a train pass by, going someplace else, and I could enjoy the going yet still be here, with the chickens and Mama and Daddy.

Maybe more than one train went by each day; that little girl's arm must have hurt, I thought. No trains ran near our place, but when I looked at the calendar, hanging above the Magic Chef stove, I could imagine that my life and the life of the black-braided girl were one. How nice it is, I thought, to spend your life waving at trains.

The fare had increased, she noticed that right away, but how long had it been since she'd taken the train to Springfield with Daddy? This was after they'd left the tiny house with the cinder backyard and the Rhode Island reds. They had moved into town. They'd gone many times to the capital, Daddy worked for the railroad and traveled free, she went half fare. Well of course it was more now. She wasn't a child now; far from it. It must have been fifty years ago, the last time they'd gone. They saw Lincoln's Tomb and Lincoln's house and the old capitol, and they always ate lunch at a coffee shop with grey formica tables across the street. Getting away from Mama, they called it; just the two of them. The trips had stopped when she was twelve and had found other things to do. As had Daddy.

She moved away for college and never came back. Until now. And here she is, on a grey March day, staring out the cloudy window of the Springfield train as it pulls away from Union Station. Miles of yards and tracks and tunnels flit by, faster now, then houses, poor people's houses, with patched shingles and junk-strewn yards. And then they breast into open country, scattered farm buildings, corn stubble breaking through patches of crusty snow. Then, way, way off, how far? A mile? Can you see a mile across Illinois prairie before horizon swallows up the landscape? Boys in heavy jackets and woolen caps, dots of red and green, running across the field, running toward the train, toward her. Waving with mittened hands and shouting. The air is cold, white plumes of breath wreathe their faces. Waving and waving. And yes, she waves back. Maybe they can see her smiling, too, as the train passes, leaving them behind.

The woman she is coming to visit is ninety-five years old. The woman was her history teacher once, for several years, a long time ago, high school. The woman is frail, feeble, losing her mind, so she's been told. But she owes this woman a last visit, commemorating acts of kindness, charity really, that the woman bestowed upon her. If not for this woman, she would not have left the state, the prairie behind.

In the taxi she took from the train, the driver has told her there are no jobs anymore. He was laid off from the Caterpillar factory before it closed down, a chemical plant will be going under, too. Welfare's up. Everything's going to China. Except me, says the driver, attempting a joke. The driver is thirty maybe, not much more. Earnest, well-spoken, and fat, a soft globular obesity made of fast food and too much cheap pop, which is what they call soda in the Midwest. The driver's vinyl seat sags and splits, straining to hold him. Where she now lives, back East, there would be no jobs for him either, maybe not even taxi driving.

The home the woman lives in is made of vinyl and imitation brick and sprawls over half an acre between a cornfield and a BP gas station. BP: does that mean the gas comes from abroad? Well, of course gasoline comes from "overseas," as they once called the rest of the world in the woman's history classes. The M_______ Home, "A Residence for the Retired" says the sign at the front, looks like a motel, except there's only one door. The woman is waiting there to meet her, supported by a staff member dressed in an oversized blue smock, grey sweat pants, navy Keds. The woman is recognizable though imploded, bones draped without concealment by slacks, a soft blue sweater meant to be enticing on someone younger. The same careful hairdo, though maybe it's a wig. Diamond earrings, incongruous she thinks, that pull at sagging pale lobes. Frail and feeble, accurate words used by the director to describe the woman. She and the director had that conversation ten days ago, she trying to determine if the woman would in fact be able to recognize her. "Still has her sight. Apparently," said the director, which did not discourage her from coming.

She reaches to embrace the woman, and closes her arms around a bag of dried leaves.

The attendant thinks she can handle this and disappears, leaving her to walk the woman, we will call her Mary, to what the attendant calls the apartment. They make their way down a long hall smelling of new carpet. Mary shuffles along, held upright by a little cart she pushes. The home isn't unpleasant, not really; they've made an effort, she can tell. Blue walls to soothe, adorned with pastel landscapes. Small wreaths of pastel plastic flowers on some of the doors, women's rooms. Sadness is contained, poignant vignettes glimpsed through doors left ajar: a crumpled man dozing in a wheelchair, his worn leather golf bag propped in a corner. Mary has, had money, she remembers. Dresses from Field's, drove a Buick back when. Gave her a Pringle cashmere sweater as a graduation gift. She remembers postcards from vacations in Japan, Rio, Rome. This must be the best that money can buy in Springfield.

Mary stops before a door marked 17; it has no wreath. Resisting assistance, Mary fumbles with a brass key dangling from a curly plastic bracelet and manages, with surprising dexterity, to open the lock. She follows Mary into a living room personalized with what must be family pieces: a camelback sofa, several upholstered chairs, a handsome antique desk. A week's worth of *Tribunes* are stacked on the coffee table. Mary, she remembers, was a devout Republican, though the paper's once-rabid politics have mellowed.

There are photographs on the desk, relatives she guesses. She points to one, a small boy, three at most, a recent color snapshot.

"My niece," says Mary.

"Great-nephew, don't you mean?"

"Her name is Judy," Mary insists, an angry edge to her voice.

"But this is a picture—" She stops herself.

She asks about another photo, this one black-and-white. A man and a woman, middle-aged, wearing large hats, both of them. Ca. 1940, she guesses. "My parents," Mary says. That's certainly possible, she thinks, doing the math in her head. "I keep it there to remind me."

"Remind you?"

"Remind me what they look like, of course." Rising impatience. "I want to be able to recognize them."

She must look puzzled, or skeptical. "In heaven, of course," snaps Mary, looking at her in a way that suggests she has lost her mind.

She has brought lotion, from the Crabtree & Evelyn in Water Tower Place. A soft floral scent, to smooth into withered hands. Mary, perched stiffly on the edge of a wing chair, wants none of it. With a shrug, she puts the bottle on the coffee table. She picks up a *Trib*, volunteers to read it aloud. No to that, too. How about a book? she asks, reaching for *Lives of the First Ladies*, sitting on the desk. It had been her present to Mary a few years ago, before Mary moved to the home. But Mary shakes her head and glowers.

She has traveled more than a thousand miles, counting the flight to O'Hare. It will be nearly two hours before the taxi returns.

"I came down here on the train, you know."

Mary looks past her, unresponding.

"The train from Chicago. There were children, boys, playing in the fields as the train passed. We waved at each other. Did you do that when you were a child, wave at trains going by?" Mary grew up here, she remembers; Mary had been a country girl.

"I've lived long enough on this earth," Mary says, by way of reply.

And then someone knocks. The attendant, who pokes her head around the door, removing any necessity for response. "Time for lunch, Miss C______, and bring your friend."

The attendant leads them to a large, high-ceilinged room with a stage at one end that must double as an auditorium. In grade school, in the Fifties, they were called multipurpose rooms and had basketball hoops. Old people, aged into neutral gender, sit at several dozen scattered card tables, many in wheelchairs. No one seems to be talking. She follows Mary and the attendant, stepping over canes and crutches, conscious of stares. Their table is on the rim, she notices. The stares are neither friendly nor curious. Nor overtly hostile, for that matter. We are beyond their consciousness, she concludes. They are served by attendants, minority women in pink polyester and hairnets who bring overdressed salads of iceberg lettuce and canned olives, white underdone sausages on whiter buns, syruped carrots, canned peach halves for dessert. She leaves the sausage untouched, declines the peaches. Mary picks at the bun and eats half a peach.

Over coffee Mary becomes more loquacious, snorting "Some food, huh?" followed abruptly by a commentary on a few of the other diners. "That fellow over there, the one with the red-checked shirt," nodding at someone behind her, "he used to be a judge." She doesn't turn, wishing not to appear rude. "And the woman beside him, she's a psychologist. Her husband was here, too, but he's dead." And Mary names more, doctors, lawyers, professors. In other words, this is a high-end place, with classy people: professionals live here, not your average riffraff. When a small Afroed woman moves to clear Mary's place, Mary gives her a surly look and doesn't say thank you.

You have become quite disagreeable, she thinks, wondering why she has made this journey. She has come to Chicago on business; the long side trip to Springfield, more than three hours on the local, had been meant as a gesture. But it was something else, too, she knows. I am looking for kindness, approbation. Encouragement. Things Mary gave me when I was young, hopeful, eager. When I waved at trains.

The old woman mindlessly stirring her coffee, rendered mute by sorrow, depression, anger, has nothing more to give.

Excusing herself to use the restroom, she calls the taxi company and asks them to come now, as soon as possible. "Twenty minutes," says the taxi man. The home is far from the center of town. Too far to walk. But she'll still be able to visit Lincoln's house, the new library, stroll around the old capitol. The Tomb is a trip she has no time for this afternoon, before the train returns her to Chicago.

Back in the dining room Mary sits at the table, staring grimly ahead. The diners are leaving, making their way to the lounge down another hall. Teenagers, members of a local church group, are here to play bingo with the residents. Mary insists on getting up without assistance. Reattaching herself to the cart, Mary moves toward the door. She follows awkwardly, aware of the eyes of other residents. A sweet-faced woman, fiftyish maybe, surely too young to be living here, smiles at her and says hello. The woman's using canes, the kind with elbow sockets. MS perhaps, or something else terminal. "Can you join us for bingo?" the woman asks. "Pah!" says Mary, scowling. She thanks the woman, trying to be gracious. Some other time.

The attendant appears. "You ladies maybe wanna play bingo?" "Pah!" says Mary again. The attendant doesn't seem surprised.

"My taxi's coming soon."

Mary doesn't respond.

"Mary, I have to leave you now."

"Say goodbye to the nice lady," prompts the attendant.

"A picture. Could you take our picture?" She pulls a small camera from her purse and hands it to the attendant. "Take two."

They huddle together, Mary and the former student no longer remembered. The camera flashes once, a second time. They move toward the door. A taxi has just pulled up, the same one that brought her there. She hugs Mary, receiving neither response nor resistance, and she is out the door and in the taxi and driving away before she remembers that she never said goodbye.

Another Time, Another Place

Bea and Phil, everyone called them that, were fifty-something when Bea taught with Geoffrey at the state college, a former teacher-training school. Phil was a self-described leather artist. He made belts and earrings and wrist cuffs from cowhide, and sold them at a craft store owned by hippies in town. Phil had been something else before, something to do with his hands, a skilled laborer maybe. Years ago he had come along with Bea, "a package deal," Bea said with a flippant laugh, from out west, but not the coast, the inner west, one of those states with lots of space where people get lost, sometimes on purpose. Bea had been a grade school teacher before she earned her doctorate, at a place I'd never heard of. Now she taught Shakespeare.

Two of their children were boys, grown, one in the army and far away, the other living on welfare in Haight-Ashbury. Bea didn't try to hide it: "Heck, we've paid our taxes all these years, about time somebody got the benefit." The middle child was a daughter, Sylvie, mother of three. Fathered by a street person in Portland, met during Sylvie's living-rough period. Bea and Phil's sons had never visited their parents, as far as anyone could tell. But now here came Sylvie, with the children, via Greyhound. En route east, said Bea. Sylvie had decided, after years of trying to find herself, that she wanted to sing, be an opera star. Sylvie was enrolling in music school, and Bea and Phil were going to pay for it, Bea said.

Bea and Phil had a party for Sylvie. Geoffrey and I were invited. Bea and Phil lived sort of rough themselves, in what had once been the mayor's house on the edge of town, a once grand Victorian now dank and dilapidated. Unruly curls of dark blue paint sprang from the siding, broken bits of gingerbread trim clung to the eaves like rotting teeth. Inside, mangy slipcovered armchairs and a camelback sofa had been shredded by their six cats, carelessly painted orange crates served as endtables, books were piled high along walls in no particular order; the carpets, of undecipherable pattern, were filthy. An unmistakable smell of feline urine hung heavily in the air, unmasked by Bea's scented candles perched precariously on the orange crates and stacks of books. We'd been there before; Bea and Phil hosted the English department on a regular basis and Geoffrey said we had to go to their parties. Bea, it seems, was influential in handing out committee assignments. She also ran the college literary magazine and had already promised to publish two of Geoffrey's poems, though this was only his second year in the department.

Geoffrey said he liked Bea. This was not surprising; he liked anyone who took him seriously. Geoffrey took himself very seriously, and had so for as long as I'd known him. One sign of his self-seriousness was his name: originally Jeffrey, he had changed the spelling in grad school, thinking it looked weightier, less frivolous. As a child, he'd been called Jeff, which he despised. Bea called him Geoffrey, of course, and more often than I thought was absolutely necessary. Bea talked nonstop, at her own and other people's parties, and Geoffrey, the same age as her younger son, she informed him at their first meeting, was a favored audience for her loud monologues on life, art, and the Elizabethans, accompanied by shoulder pats, lapel straightening, repetitive arm squeezes.

Bea had little use for me. I worked part-time in the library and had not finished an undergraduate degree. "Oh, but you *sound* like a college graduate!" Bea trumpeted when we first met, implying the opposite. Bea was a wheedler, and on this occasion she had pried from me every piece of personal information she could. She didn't like it that I'd gone to an eastern college, a girls' school. She thought women's colleges were too limited, and limiting, and said so. I knew she didn't like me and I said so to Geoffrey, but he told me I was feeling unnecessarily inferior, or was it superior, and to snap out of it.

Bea and Phil were real people, Geoffrey said, they hadn't sold out to the establishment was how he put it, look how they went once a month to Columbus, and at their age too, protesting the war. (Geoffrey's admiration did not inspire imitation; he was not a war protestor himself.) I wondered what good it did to march against the war at the state capitol, and I doubted Bea's academic skills after Geoffrey told me her students made models of the Globe Theatre for their senior project. But what did I know? I wasn't a college graduate.

Tonight Sylvie was holding court in one of the armchairs, in a far corner of the living room, and Bea pulled us over to meet her while Phil got the drinks. Draped in an orange-flowered muu-muu, oversized tortoise-rimmed glasses slipping down her nose, Bea pushed through knots of department faculty plus a few extras from psych and poli sci I recognized from the library. "Make way, make way!" she boomed, and the crowd parted without hesitation. Bea was a large woman with a big head accentuated by what had to be a wig, an improbably shiny blondish-brown, improbably tidy, tightly rolled in the flip-and-fold style of the late Sixties. Bea was used to being in charge. Phil was smaller, without force or pretension. He was ill at ease with academic types. Between stints tending bar for Bea, he'd retreat to the den and watch sit-coms. I rather liked him, and I think he liked me. Which gave Bea even more reason to view me with distaste.

Sylvie also wore a flowing garment, off-white cotton splattered with watery blue blotches, tie-dye was the fashion then in some circles, and silver-toned rings on her fingers. Her green eyes were ringed with kohl, like Isak Dinesen's. She'd tied a faded bandana around her dark curls. Wispy feathers, dyed pink, the kind on those Kewpie dolls you got for winning the ring toss at a street carnival, dangled on gold hoops from her ears. Unclean bare feet peeked out from the hem of her dress. One of the cats sat on her lap, cleaning its anus. "And here is my famous prodigy," said Bea, drawing Geoffrey closer. Sylvie smiled at him and patted the arm of the oversized chair, inviting him to sit. Which he did. They began to chat. He was asking her about her career when I wandered off to the kitchen, in search of a drink and other company.

"What does she plan to do with the children?" I said to him later that night, back home. We were getting ready for bed. I asked for the sake of conversation, nothing else. I had hardly seen him all evening. I wanted to make a connection.

"How the hell should I know?" Geoffrey snapped. "Why is that so important?"

He was angry. I hadn't been too sociable at the party is how he put it. We had had that conversation in the car driving home. I wasn't being a good faculty spouse, chatting up the department chairman's wife and begging her to share her recipe for the lime sherbet punch we'd so enjoyed at their Christmas open house. Instead I spent the evening talking to Phil about leather decoration before I was cornered by the department joke, an assistant professor of English pedagogy for nearly forty years, McAdams I think was his name. He collected soda bottle caps. He had, he told me in a confidential tone, probably the largest collection of Moxies in the country if not the world. "There you go wasting your time again," said Geoffrey. And now I was trying to change the subject.

I had seen the children that evening, packed away in a room upstairs. Stumbling down the dark hall looking for the toilet I opened a bedroom door by mistake. A dim yellow light shone on three tiny bodies curled up asleep on a large bed, unwashed, unkempt, their hair stringy and matted. One of them, a little girl, sucked intermittently on a lollipop, the kind on a loop of string, plopped in her mouth like a pacifier. Alongside her an older boy, maybe four, in dirty underpants, clutched a scrap of blanket. The third was a fat baby, wrapped up tightly in a soiled sheet and tied to the headboard so it wouldn't roll off the bed. The smell of urine, both cat and baby, was strong. I stepped back out in the hall and there was Bea. "Looking for the bathroom," I said. "Sorry."

"They're Sylvie's," Bea replied. "Their daddy doesn't want them so Sylvie had to bring them on."

I tried again with Geoffrey, though I didn't look at him. I was sitting on the side of the bed, stripping off pantyhose. "They're still babies. How can she go to school and take care of three little children?"

"We didn't discuss it," said Geoffrey. He was already in bed, and now he snapped off the light, mumbled goodnight, and turned on his side, away from me.

Phil and Bea, Bea and Phil, The Twosome, they called themselves, or rather Bea did. Phil didn't say much about the personal side of things.

They had pictures of themselves tacked up in the kitchen. They'd met after high school, Bea said, and the photos began with the young black-and-white, prewar Bea and Phil posing stiffly behind a cake topped by a tiny bridal pair. "The cake wasn't ours," said Bea over my shoulder, when she caught me staring the first time Geoffrey and I came over. "Just plaster-of-paris, or whatever they used back then. We got married in Vegas. By a JP. Nineteen-thirty-two. Honeymooned in Tijuana. A dump." Her laugh didn't sound funny.

"You don't look—"

"Of course we don't look the same. Nobody does. We were different people then, Phil and I." She pushed me aside to get more ice from the freezer.

More pictures. Phil in a sailor suit; he'd been in the navy during the war. Bea and Phil with some much older people standing in front of a tile-roofed adobe, flanked by cacti; parents? Phil and Bea, this one in color, at a beach, under a big blue umbrella; their faces were shadowed but you knew it was Phil and Bea. I hadn't been about to say she looked different. *You don't look happy*, that's what I almost blurted out. Now they were older, much older, and Bea wore a Dynel wig to hide what must have been sparse gray hair and Phil was nearly bald and Bea had grown fat and Phil too lean, but they were still the same people. You'd know them anywhere.

There were no pictures of children.

At breakfast the next morning, it was Saturday, Geoffrey announced he was driving to Toledo. "And then maybe Detroit, if we can't find what we need."

I didn't ask if I could ride along. I had to work at the library in the afternoon, though I'm not sure Geoffrey knew this, or remembered.

"A project?" I asked. "You and Denny?" Denny Strait taught pedagogy, a fancy word for teacher training. He worked on the newer stuff, felt boards, AV presentations, things McAdams couldn't or wouldn't learn how to do. Geoffrey had three sections of American lit, surveys: "Self-Reliance," a few Poe poems, a Hawthorne short story, and if the class was really bright, he said, he threw in *Turn of the Screw* and maybe an early Bellow, *Seize the Day*, if there was time. He and Denny had teamed up last semester to do a slide show on *Moby Dick*. The kids have to know the story, Geoffrey said, without apparent irony.

Geoffrey had written his dissertation on the later novels of Henry James. His director had three degrees from Harvard and was fairly well-known, though relegated, through politics Geoffrey said, to a second-tier university in California. Geoffrey had not been happy to come to a fourth-tier college in Ohio. Politics again, said Geoffrey. But he was trying to make the best of it. Developing other specialties, he said, that's what he had to do. There was his poetry, sent out to all the good little magazines and rhythmically returned, without comment. And there was film, foreign film, cinema was getting academic attention now—why not be an expert on Kurosawa, Fellini, etc. etc. All he had to do was publish a few articles in *Cahiers*, never mind that he didn't know French, they had translators, get on a panel at MLA. And then the big places, Cornell maybe, or Penn at the very least, would come calling.

It wasn't me he was mad at. He was angry with himself.

I poured him a second cup of coffee and slipped two slices of Pepperidge Farm whole wheat—I had to drive eight miles to buy it—into the toaster. Geoffrey was eating fried eggs on Wonder Bread. "You're going with Denny, right?" I asked again.

He looked uncomfortable. "Bea asked me to do her a favor . . . "

"You're driving Bea again?" I tried not to sound judgmental. Phil didn't drive because Bea didn't want him to, he was getting too old, she said. And Bea didn't like to drive herself without Phil along. And Phil had to do his leatherwork and wasn't always available. Bea and Phil, Phil and Bea. Geoffrey often drove Bea somewhere.

We lived two miles from the library. It was raining. I needed the car.

"It's Sylvie I'm taking," he said. "Music. She needs some sheet music. Bea asked me if I wouldn't mind."

"And Bea's not going because she has to look after the children?"

"I was thinking—"

"That I'd do it? I have to work this afternoon. And I need the car. Maybe you can take Bea's?"

Bea's Plymouth wagon was in the shop, getting new brakes. Bea had papers to grade. I called the library, and they told me it was okay, don't come in, no one's around anyway. Geoffrey went over to Bea's and brought the kids back to our house, and then he drove off.

They weren't bad kids, as children go. Personally I am not fond of children. I was an only child myself. I didn't go to the playground much, polio being in season during my early years. I never learned to play. I preferred adults.

But here they were, dirty, tear-stained, confused. Ricky, the eldest, wearing stiff blue jeans and a stained Superman T-shirt, clutched the blanket scrap I'd seen him sleeping with the night before. Daisy, in a torn blue dress a size too small, carried a wrinkled brown paper bag. "Suckers," she said, offering cherry lollipops. The baby, Moira, was just beginning to walk. Worn plastic pants, heavy with soaked diapers, sagged down her chubby legs. Above her diapers she wore a ripped pink shirt with a faded Tweetie-bird stencil on the front.

Sylvie, or Bea, had sent along a shopping bag: diapers, a dime-store coloring book, a six-pack of generic crayons, three or four plastic toys, the kind they gave away at gas stations. At the bottom of the bag were several bottles of prescription syrup, Ricky's, and a sippy cup.

"You need this now?" I asked Ricky, showing him the bottles. He shook his head and stuck a thumb in his mouth. I looked at the labels: asthma medicine.

I couldn't love them. You can't love someone else's problems, can you? You can pity; but pity isn't the same as love. What you can give is attention. Motivated, you might say, by enlightened self-interest. Suffering, disorder, casual cruelty, they all affront. So I led them into the bathroom and turned on the taps in the chipped claw-foot tub. They were docile children, they let me undress them without a murmur. Ricky's legs and torso were spotted with what looked like insect bites, small scabbed sores. Or was it impetigo; I remembered having it once, as a child, though not like this. Or maybe something more sinister: cigarette burns. Moira, not surprisingly, had severe diaper rash. Daisy, quite surprisingly, seemed unmarred, though her hair was the stickiest. I lifted them into the shallow tub and told Ricky to hold onto Moira while I dumped their clothes in the washer just off the kitchen.

I bathed them as gently as I could, working old dirt out of tight crevices, patting Ricky's wounds warily. The children seemed in a trance, their eyes half-closed, undulating slightly, like purring cats, when I let streams of warm water cascade down their backs. I had to use Prell on their hair, and I showed Ricky and Daisy how to hold the washcloth so it wouldn't get in their eyes and make them sting. Ricky held the cloth for Moira while I washed her small tufted head.

Bundling Ricky and Daisy in bath towels, I sat them on the sofa while I diapered Moira. I had a small collection of children's books, mine, stacked on a lower shelf flanking the fireplace. *The Tall Book of Nursery Tales* was there, and another Rojankovsky, *The Tall Book of Mother Goose*, and the Volland *Mother Goose* as well, and *Ring o' Roses*, and *Leslie Brooke's Children's Book.* Old-fashioned, whimsical books, with prickly humor and a cheerfulness that didn't cloy.

I showed them to the children. Ricky, sucking his thumb, looked at me but said nothing. Moira picked silently at the piping on the slipcover. But Daisy spoke up. "That one," she said, pointing to *Nursery Tales*. So I sat down with them, Ricky on my right, Daisy on the left, Moira wrapped in an afghan on my lap, and we read, I did, starting with "Little Red Riding Hood." Their clothes whirled in the dryer, and a faint contrapuntal *ping* from Ricky's jean studs shadowed my voice. Moira fell asleep soon after we started "The Foolish Milkmaid," but Ricky and Daisy, though they said nothing, looked intently at the pictures. When the buzzer rang, and a last *ping* sounded, we had gotten as far as "The Three Big Sillies." Ricky released his thumb and pointed at the picture of the man jumping into his pants hooked to the dresser drawer. "Daddy," he said. "That's my daddy."

I fed them a late lunch, Campbell's Chicken Noodle Soup, peanut butter crackers, carrot sticks, mashed banana and yogurt for Moira. They ate everything quickly and wanted more. I wondered if they'd had any breakfast. They needed naps, I decided. They were still wrapped in towels, I hadn't put their clothes back on, and I found two shrunken T-shirts, set aside for Goodwill, for Ricky and Daisy. I changed Moira, rewrapped her in the afghan (crocheted from parti-colored Woolworth's yarn by Geoffrey's mother), and carried her into our bedroom, Geoffrey's and mine. We had a small house, rented from the college; the other bedroom was Geoffrey's study. Ricky and Daisy followed me and lay down at my direction on the bed. The yellow chenille cover was old;

they couldn't harm it. I settled Moira, dozing off again, between them and shut the door.

It was late May, I needed to work in the garden—it had stopped raining—but I didn't want to go outside and leave them. Something might happen. The baby could fall off the bed (though little harm would come to her; it wasn't very high off the floor). Ricky, who seemed the least stable, or most spooked, take your pick, of the three, could have an asthma attack and I wouldn't hear him in time. And it was supposed to be a library afternoon anyway.

I scrubbed out the tub, using extra Comet to loosen the children's dirt sticking to the worn surface. I mopped the floor. I looked for raisins in the cupboard and baked cookies. I clipped a recipe for lime Jell-O mold, the kind with walnuts and pineapple, from the *Blade*, and Happy Homemaker menu suggestions for the perfect Memorial Day picnic: deviled eggs, *check*, three-bean salad, *check*, beet slaw, something new. I clipped that recipe, too. You had to work at adjusting yourself to the Midwest, at least that was my experience. Food, a certain kind of food, was important. Premixed, boxed or canned; fresh vegetables, when used, cooked to extinction; ditto meat. I had grown up in California, eating everything fresh.

Geoffrey, as Jeffrey, had a different upbringing. A small town in Washington State, near the river. The kind of home where thick clear plastic covered the living room furniture. His father worked as a foreman in a lumber mill. His mother was, as they said then, a homemaker. She gave me a Betty Crocker cookbook as a wedding present. She was prescient; it came in handy when we left California.

I slipped the Jell-O recipe into the "Salads" section of the Betty Crocker and stuck the other clippings on the Amana door with magnets. Geoffrey liked this kind of food; seeing the recipes would please him, I figured.

The children started waking up about four, Daisy first. She came out to the kitchen, holding onto Ricky's blanket scrap that I'd retrieved from the dryer before his nap. "Up now," she said, rubbing her flushed face. It was furrowed from the bedspread. "No more sleep." Ricky staggered out after her and snatched the blanket back, but this did not provoke a response from Daisy. I went in to retrieve Moira before she could fall. Her diaper felt heavy with urine inside the plastic pants, which I'd tried to wash out by hand when they'd all had their baths. What else did babies do besides eat and pee? Except this time she'd also had a bowel movement. Repressing a gag, I laid her down on the kitchen floor and wiped her off with paper towels while Daisy and Ricky looked on without comment.

They must not have had Sylvie's music in Toledo. They must have driven up to Detroit.

I got the children dressed in their cleaned clothes and fed them cookies and orange juice. Moira drank hers from the sippy cup. I am getting reasonably good at this, I thought, congratulating myself on benevolence. On the other hand, I did not like children, did I, and Geoffrey made it clear before we were married that he didn't want any. And this was only a matter of hours, after all, a suspension of the children's ordinary life. Here they were mesmerized, bemused by care and concern. Adjusted, inured to a kindly upbringing, they would change, become normal, energized, rowdy beings who needed constant supervision. Every day for years and years. Hormones and acne following hard on the heels of pee and vomit. I could not deal with that day in and day out.

Moira tipped the sippy cup into her mouth without a spill, Ricky and Daisy ate their cookies carefully, wasting no crumbs, and I slipped into what Geoffrey once called my fugue state, a kind of trance in which I was there and somewhere else, too. The somewhere else was years before, six, two before we got married.

We were meeting for the first time. Geoffrey was about to start graduate school at the university in my hometown. I was back from college for the summer and had a job in the admissions office. Geoffrey came in to see about something, it might have been his transcript from the small school he'd attended in western Washington. I had to find his file. I was wearing a blue linen skirt and matching blouse, there were still dress codes then, in offices, and a pair of new slingback heels made of supple white calfskin, from I. Magnin. Geoffrey was attractive, in a wholesome, well-scrubbed sort of way. I was attracted. I was barely twenty, with no idea of what I would do after college. Mother said it was a big mistake, I was too young, I should graduate and then find a more suitable person, meaning someone with better prospects, banking maybe, or at least a law student, but I married him nonetheless, eloping as Phil and Bea had done. And had no regrets, none that I would admit to, not until now anyway.

It was after five o'clock. The phone rang. It was Bea. She wondered if I could keep the children a bit longer; the car hadn't been fixed and she had no way to get them. She didn't seem at all surprised that Geoffrey wasn't back yet. "Lots to see in Detroit, this is Sylvie's first time there."

I wondered what, exactly, might be interesting to Sylvie in Detroit. Hudson's Department Store? The zoo? The burned-out ghetto? True, there were all those quaint little markets and hippie shops and ethnic cafés where people worked who looked just like her. We'd made the tour with Bea and Phil soon after our arrival two years earlier. I bought baklava and a pair of earrings. Geoffrey thought it was dirty and uninteresting. At least that's what he said then.

She knew I had no plans; where could I go without a car? The movies maybe, a Quonset hut showing B pictures half a mile out on the highway. "Sure," I said. "I hope I have enough diapers."

"You can always rip up some old sheets," she said, and hung up.

Geoffrey came in the house at ten-thirty, give or take a minute. The children were dozing on the sofa. We'd watched *Cinderella*, or tried to, on the thirteen-inch TV. In black and white, on a small screen, it was hard to keep their attention.

"You're back," I said inanely, looking at my watch.

"Yeah. So let's get the kids in the car. I'll run them over to Bea and Phil's."

"Where's Sylvie?"

"Waiting," he said, and moved toward the sofa.

I got Ricky up, then Daisy, who started to cry. I hoisted sleeping Moira over my shoulder and headed outside.

We put the kids in the backseat. The car smelled of beer. Sylvie, asleep, or maybe drunk and passed out, was slumped in the front. Daisy howled but Sylvie gave no sign she heard.

I was in the kitchen when he got back, washing out the sink. "Sorry, but there's no dinner saved. It was hamburgers, the kids ate them."

He ignored this, opened the refrigerator and pulled out a Heineken. I'd changed his tastes in beer at least. I started to ask haven't you had enough but decided not to.

"So," I said instead, hanging up the dishtowel neatly, so that the corners met, "did you find it? Sylvie's music?"

"Yes," he said. "We did." He fished around in the gadget drawer by the sink for the bottle opener. He smelled of something else besides beer. Sandalwood, musk, odors of dimly lit little stores that sold candles and incense and Indian bedspreads.

"Well, we had a pretty nice day, the kids and I," I said brightly, sitting down at the kitchen table. It had a marbleized grey Formica top, chrome-rimmed, and chrome tube legs, and an extra leaf in the middle. The tube-legged chairs had small back and seat cushions covered in red vinyl. Bea had found the set for us, second-hand, at a yard sale soon after we'd moved in. Geoffrey liked it because it reminded him of home.

Geoffrey leaned against the sink, drinking from the bottle. He looked neat, clean, well-pressed, despite the long day and the smells, no wrinkles in his blue madras shirt and khaki pants. He'd worn a crewcut in California; now his blondish hair curled around his ears but it still looked tidy.

"They all had a good time, I think."

Either Geoffrey wasn't in a talking mood or he was trying to figure out what he was going to say, I couldn't tell which. He drank, sighed, turned the bottle in his hands, made a pretense of reading the label.

"Do you like her?" I asked at last. "Do you like her very much?"

He looked at me then and said, "Yes. Yes, I do."

In grad school Geoffrey had been a teaching assistant. He had slept with two, maybe three of his students. This was while we were dating, before we eloped. I was upset at first when I found out, by then I thought of us as a couple, but he said it shouldn't worry me, this was just getting it all out of his system before we got married. Men were like that, he said; women were different. After marriage it would be just the two of us. But it wasn't.

Marriage made me wan and apathetic. Four years on, I was drifting, moving about without any clear purpose. Work in the library, Geoffrey directed, so I got a job as a circulation clerk. Join the faculty wives' club, which I did and went to monthly coffees at other homes and hid in the bathrooms while the women gossiped. Plant tomatoes, tomatoes grow well here, so I did that too, even though the surplus from the Heinz catsup factory on the edge of town sold for a nickel a pound in August. Bea, of course, provided the plants. Geoffrey's fanciful destinations, *Cahiers* and Cornell and those little magazines, grew more remote, I could see that, yet I went on drifting, without the inclination to set a course for myself.

Sylvie changed that. And Bea, of course. In retrospect, they did me a big favor.

Sylvie got in at Eastman, she must have had some talent. Geoffrey drove her there the following weekend, with the children. He took Bea's car. He had spent the week at Bea and Phil's, telling me it was the right thing to do as he packed up socks and underwear and his good suit, the one he always wore to MLA. "You've changed," he told me, zipping up the canvas suitcase. We'd shared it on our two-day honeymoon at Lake Tahoe. "But we all do. No one ever stays the same. Not for long."

He came back for two weeks, to finish up his classes. And then moved east for good.

Bea, when I saw her, was full of apologies. I'd turned down the dairy aisle at the Foodtown and there she was, opening a carton of eggs, looking for cracks. I couldn't retreat, someone was behind me, and I couldn't move around her unseen, either. She looked up and saw me and drew back, momentarily startled. So sorry, didn't see it coming, what must I think of her, think of Bea and Phil, they didn't believe in breaking up marriages, of course not.

I let her babble on a few minutes more. Bobby Kennedy had just been shot. He was clinging to life. Such a tragedy for the antiwar movement, she said. I nodded assent, wished her good day and moved on.

I ran into Phil a few weeks later, pumping gas at the Standard station. I came in to have a tire replaced on the old Rambler—Geoffrey had left it behind, preferring Sylvie's used but newer Mustang, a gift from her parents. The leather business was slow, Phil said; not many sales in the summer, when the students went home. He needed another job then. On impulse, I asked after the grandchildren. How were they doing, I wanted to know, Ricky, Daisy, little Moira? I'd enjoyed taking care of them, I said, which wasn't entirely untrue.

Phil shook his head and dropped his voice. "Sylvie put them all in foster care," he said.

I didn't ask about Geoffrey.

(I look back over what I have written. Have I been too hard on Geoffrey? Snotty, certainly: all that business about his family being low-end, plastic-covered, Betty Crockered. I have to give Geoffrey credit: he had no social pretensions. Intellectual, yes. But not social. True, he traded Pabst for Heineken's, but he shopped at Sears and Penney's and preferred fast food. And always spoke of his hardworking parents with respect. I have to say I admired that.)

Twenty years on. It's the Eighties, and I've long since pulled myself together, as they say. Though I haven't changed, not really. Having a little money helped, my grandmother's money that had paid for college, and a home to go back to for a while. Mother, to her credit, did not berate me for making a marriage she had opposed. Instead she urged me forward, and I went back to the New England college that Bea thought was limited/limiting. I graduated, and finished grad school too. I am not an ambitious person, but I needed to earn a living, and so I've been teaching at a small, undistinguished college in upstate New York for nearly a decade. Purely by coincidence it's a hundred miles or so from Rochester and Eastman. I have never been to Rochester.

Geoffrey and I have been divorced for most of that time and have not kept in touch, as they say. I do not know where he lives or what he is doing. I am single. I live alone, in a modest clapboard house surrounded by perennial gardens. The neighbors, themselves academics, admire my lilacs each spring. Once a year, during winter break, I spend two weeks in Manhattan, going to plays, operas, recitals, and sleeping with a fellow history professor, a pleasant older man who teaches at a small college in Pennsylvania and has as little ambition as I do; I met him at a conference some years ago. He is a longtime widower; I have confirmed this personal information; no one, as far as I can tell, is being hurt by our relationship. We have no wish to marry, and I assume he sleeps with other people as he pleases. I do not.

For the record, I have followed the classical music scene rather closely over these twenty years in question. I have seen no mention of any Sylvie S_______—or P_______, Geoffrey's surname, for that matter. Though perhaps she has changed her name to something else entirely.

On this day in September, twenty years after Geoffrey left me, I am looking over the list of students for my freshman history class. I have just been handed the list by the department chairman before entering the classroom, and now I stand at the lectern and start to call the names. There are twenty-some students, male and female, slouched in rows before me, exhibiting varying degrees of disinterest. Apathetic yeses confirm their presence when I read their names. I am almost at the end as I call "Moira S________." I look up at the sound of her voice, and there is baby Moira, all grown up, sitting in the third row, four desks back.

People don't change. You know them anywhere.

She looks like her mother, or am I imagining this? Dark ringlets caught up in a scarf, large light-blue eyes (kohl-free; that's not the style anymore). Levi's instead of tie-dye, but the Mexican peasant blouse could have been Sylvie's. Dr. Scholl's clogs. She's rather attractive, and more attentive than most of the other students, if one can rely on body language: she's sitting up and looking straight at me, not draped languorously across the desk.

All the while I pass out syllabi and outline the semester and explain my grading practice, I'm wondering if I will say something to her. Not today necessarily, but maybe later. The semester lasts sixteen weeks. I have time.

She is a good student, by which I mean she attends class regularly, gives me her full attention during each period, answers when called upon, turns assignments in on time, and gets a B-plus on her first quiz (the class average is a very low C). Four weeks have passed, and I have said nothing to her about her life outside the classroom. I am biding my time.

She wouldn't know me, she has no reason to. I have a common first name. I gave up Geoffrey's surname after the divorce.

Perhaps I am wrong, after all. Perhaps this is not the same Moira, my Moira.

(My Moira, that's how I've come to think of her, *my* Moira should be finishing college now, not enrolled as a freshman.)

If I were an English teacher, I could assign personal essays. *My Worst Memories. What I Admire Least About My Parents. My Thoughts on Adultery.* But that wouldn't be appropriate in American History 101.

And if it is my Moira, what would I say? Invite her out for coffee? Compare scars? That is not my nature.

Still, her identity should be confirmed.

I check her enrollment card in the bursar's office.

Place of birth: Portland, Oregon. *Check.*

Year of birth: 1967. *Check.*

Her parents' names are not listed. Beside *Guardian or Closest Relative* someone has typed a woman's name I don't recognize, an address in Greece, New York. A town outside Rochester. Bingo.

And then she vanishes. On the day of midterms she doesn't show up for class. Or the next day or the next.

I call the bursar. He tells me she's withdrawn from the college.

I should have made an effort. I should have called the woman, no doubt her foster mother, in Greece, New York. I owed her that. I owed them all something, Ricky and Daisy as well as Moira. I should have spoken to her before she disappeared. I should have protested, screamed with outrage when Geoffrey packed his suitcase. I should have gone to Bea and Phil and said you cannot do this, let your daughter run off with my husband. He doesn't want children, he'll give them away, you'll never see your grandchildren again. *Doesn't that matter?* But they would not have listened. Bea would have smiled and told me not to be hysterical, it didn't suit me, she had me pegged as the passive type, I never marched with them in Columbus, did I, and Geoffrey told them that was why he didn't go either, because I didn't want to, and Phil would have skulked into the den to watch *I Love Lucy* reruns.

It would have done no good.

Recently I read in the paper that people say they are less happy the older they are. Hardly startling news. Youth equals bliss born of self-delusion and ignorance. In old age we know too much, and the self-knowledge we possess is painful to contemplate. Depression ultimately paralyzes will, and we become versions of Phil, retreating to self-obscuring corners.

I'm retired now, and have, as it were, time on my hands. I take long walks with the dog, an abandoned terrier rescued from the pound, and on those walks I linger in front of the stores that cater to students in our town. The dog was my doctor's suggestion, to get me out of the house. I'm aging and live alone; I stopped making annual trips to New York years ago, after the death of my sometime lover. I read about it in a history journal.

The town and the college have both grown since I first came here. Yesterday I passed an older, graying man, wearing rimless spectacles and a denim apron, sitting in a shop window braiding a leather belt. This was something new. The place used to be a shoe store but closed a few months ago; too much competition from the chains out on the highway.

Bunches of young people milled about, jostling and joking, licking ice cream cones, listening to iPods. It's June but students don't leave anymore, they stay for summer school. I crossed the street with the dog and sat us both on a bench in front of the drugstore. I pretended to read a *Times* I'd picked up earlier at Starbucks, all the while keeping an eye on the shop with the Leatherman, as I'd dubbed him. No one went in, no one looked in the window, no one paid any attention.

Half an hour went by. I recrossed the street. I tied the dog's leash to the parking meter outside the shop. I went inside. How much? I asked, pointing to a wallet he was now polishing. He named a price that might or might not have been fair, and I followed him to the cash register. He looked younger inside the shop, worn and used but not as old as I was. More middle-aged.

"This a present?" he asked laconically. "You want it wrapped?"

"A bag is fine," I said. Then, "Is business pretty good?"

"Not bad. So-so. People mostly buy at the mall now. I'm trying to be more high-end."

He handed me the bag and change. "Here, take one of my cards," he said. I reached for it. *R&D Leatherworks.*

"Me and my sister, we run the place."

I lingered. "You do all this work yourself?" Wooden shelves displayed handbags, belts, more wallets.

"Yeah."

"Where did you learn how?"

He looked me over and decided I might become a repeat customer. "My granddad."

"He lives around here?"

"Did once. Died. Cancer. Dyes and stuff in the leather. Mine's untreated," he said proudly. "Hides I get are local."

In a few weeks I'll return to R&D Leatherworks. I could use a new purse, and I might as well support local business. In the course of making my purchase I'll ask and be told Leatherman's name, and the name of his sister. And perhaps his grandfather, too. Confirming what I already know.

Whether I choose to reveal our mutual history remains to be seen.

About the Author

Ann T. Keene was born in Chicago and educated at Swarthmore College and Indiana University. She has lived and worked as an editor and writer in New York City, Washington DC, Los Angeles, and Zurich, and has taught literature and writing at Indiana University and George Mason University. Keene is an ongoing contributor to *American National Biography* (Oxford University Press), as well as other adult biographical reference works. She is also the author of half a dozen nonfiction books for young adults, including *Earthkeepers: Observers and Protectors of Nature* and *Peacemakers*, both published by Oxford. Her young-adult biography *Willa Cather*, originally published by Simon & Schuster, is available as a reprint through iUniverse. *Another Time, Another Place* is her first published collection of short stories. Keene, who has four grown children, lives with her husband and four Boston terriers in Princeton, New Jersey.